3

THEFT IN THE THEATER

PEARL SANDS BEACH RESORT COZY MYSTERY
BOOK THREE

DANIELLE COLLINS
MILLIE BRIGGS

Fairfield Publishing

CONTENTS

"WHOEVER SAID that event planning wasn't supposed to be stressful if you had a plan did *not* know what they were talking about." Juliana Gomez stood in the middle of the largest ballroom at the Pearl Sands Beach Resort with an armful of black and gold decorations.

"What happened?" Charlene Davis, better known as Charlie to her friends and co-workers, rushed across the dark herringbone wood floors to help the woman.

"I slipped." Juliana's tanned cheeks turned pink under Charlie's concerned gaze, and she took in a shaky breath as if moments away from crying. Charlie thought she might be.

"Are you all right?" Charlie asked.

"Yes, yes, of course, but the table decorations..." She shook her head and swallowed hard.

"Will be fine. I plan on having the staff hang some of these up high, anyway. No one will be able to see they are a little crushed." Charlie flashed a big smile at the woman.

"Are you sure? I could try to purchase replacements."

"Absolutely not." While Charlie knew the woman's heart was in the right place, she also had come to know the former maid who had become Charlie's first new hire to her concierge staff. Not only was she completely qualified for the position, but she was supporting her grandmother, sister, and three young nieces at home. Charlie knew that money was tight. Besides, accidents happened, and Charlie knew the decorations were destined to be torn down after the gala anyway.

"Go ahead and place them on that table. I'll talk with Lucas about getting them up in the next day or so. Look, I drew I diagram." Charlie proudly held out the pad of paper she'd used to roughly sketch the ballroom and where she planned on having the decorations set up.

"Very nice," Juliana said. Her color returned to normal with the shift in focus, and Charlie felt certain she had convinced her that everything would be all right. "What's next?"

Charlie checked her watch. "Looks like it's about time for us to clock out."

"Already? But we still have the rest of the tables to figure out and the seating arrangements and—"

"And we have three more days for that, remember?"

Juliana opened her mouth to protest but closed it just as quickly. "Whatever you say, Ms. Davis."

Charlie narrowed her eyes at her. "I'm going to break you of that 'Ms. Davis' habit soon. Just you wait and see."

Julianna smiled despite trying to hold it in. "It's just being respectful."

"It makes me feel old."

That made Juliana laugh. "You're not old."

"Now you're flattering me? Are you angling for a raise already? You've only worked with me for three weeks."

Juliana's eyes went wide at the insinuation. "I would never do that."

"I was teasing." Charlie realized her mistake and tempered her smile. "I like to tease, and I prefer a relaxed work environment. I'm sorry if that's coming off the wrong way." Charlie held up a hand to stay what she assumed would be the woman's protest and apology. "I'm still new at being a supervisor, so please forgive me."

Juliana took a breath. "I think I'm worried the other foot is going to drop."

Charlie frowned. "Oh, you mean shoe?"

"I— Yes. Shoe." Juliana giggled, finally relaxing somewhat. "When I approached you about the possibility of a job, I was so worried that instead I might end up without one at all. I just do not want to mess this up."

"Then relax," Charlie said, smiling down at the younger woman. "Because you're not going to."

The sound of the double-doors opening drew their attention. Felipe Delgado strode in, shoulders back and head held high like he owned the place. He didn't, but as the manager of the Pearl Sands Beach Resort, he oversaw all of its inner and outer workings and was the reason Charlie had been hired on to start the resort's new concierge program.

"Go on home," Charlie urged the woman. "I'll answer the million questions Mr. Delgado likely has for us."

Juliana looked a little shocked at Charlie's bold comments about their boss, but she nodded and scurried off to the desk she shared with Charlie in the lobby.

"Ah, Ms. Davis, how are preparations going?" Felipe wore a lightweight linen shirt over tan pants and expensive leather shoes. His salt-and-pepper hair was immaculately groomed, as was his beard, but his dark brown eyes held a hint of tiredness Charlie was surprised to see.

"They are going just as well as they were the last time you checked in—" She looked at her watch for dramatic effect. "—about twenty minutes ago."

"It was longer than that."

"All right, twenty-five." She held his gaze and offered a smile. "Are you all right?"

He looked taken aback by her observation but shrugged. "It is my mother. She is not doing well, and I have been spending more time at the facility we moved her to, but they only have one of those awful lounge chairs to sleep in. Not comfortable at all."

"I'm sorry to hear that." Charlie felt for the man. He had to balance a demanding career as well as a big event week the resort was all but hosting, plus his own family life.

A twinge of regret snagged at Charlie's heart, but she didn't let herself inspect it. Not here in the middle of a mostly empty ballroom with the man who was not only her boss but a friend.

"She is doing better, but the commute is likely to kill me as well." He let out a long sigh.

"Is there anything I can do to help?"

"No, no, no, but I do appreciate your kind offer. Truly, though, how are we doing for the event?"

Charlie pulled out her handy notepad and was about to show him her drawings when the door squeaked again.

"Sir. Sir?"

"What is it, Michael?" Felipe asked, his voice holding a tinge of barely contained frustration.

"I— I'm sorry to interrupt you and Ms. Davis here, but—"

"Michael. Tell me."

Charlie turned raised eyebrows to Felipe. He wasn't usually short with anyone on staff, but ever since the owner of the resort had insisted that he hire Michael

Adair to help with the day-to-day tasks around the resort, she'd seen Felipe trying his best to avoid the younger man.

"Right. You wanted to be updated on the arrival of *you-know-who*." Michael raised his brows in an exaggerated fashion.

"Ms. Kent and Mr. Armstrong, yes. What of it?"

"Well, they—they're—they're here."

Charlie watched as Felipe's eyes narrowed. "What are you talking about? They are scheduled to arrive tomorrow afternoon."

"I know. That's why I'm here. Their suites aren't ready, and I don't know where to put them." Michael slammed his mouth shut and blinked his large, round eyes. He looked a little like a fish, and Charlie had to keep herself from laughing at the image.

"I see." Felipe's usually calm exterior slipped back into place as if he had always expected the guests to show up early. "Charlie, would you like to meet our guests?"

Charlie frowned. "I've got a party to plan."

"My dear, don't you know?"

She frowned back at his amused expression. "Know what?"

"It's their party you're planning."

CHARLIE WAS the first to admit that she didn't keep up with social media or popular news outlets, but when she walked into the lobby of the Pearl Sands Beach Resort, she could see that she was in the minority.

Despite the evening hour that usually saw the lobby empty, it was filled with hotel staff as well as a large party —likely the ones Michael had mentioned—ready to check in.

"News spreads fast, huh, Miss Charlie?" Parker, one of the bellhops, said with a wide grin.

She shook her head. "All of this for two people?"

"Two massively *famous* people," Parker amended.

Charlie shrugged.

"You're not a fan of Katherina Kent and Elliot Armstrong?" Parker's eyes widened even while he whispered the stars' names.

"I'm sad to say I don't even know who they are."

He shook his head. "Miss Charlie, you need to get out more."

She chuckled, her head bobbing. "You're probably right. Fill me in on the basics."

"Where do I start?" He sighed dramatically, grinning at the look she gave him. "You've at least heard about the movie that's premiering here, right? *A Night of Starlight*?"

Her forehead wrinkled. "All Felipe told me was glitz and glamor."

Parker rolled his eyes to the vaulted ceiling, the gold-and-crystal chandelier no doubt blinding him from the action. "Have mercy. Okay, so it's set in the roaring twenties about an heiress who is forced to marry for political position, but her husband dies under mysterious circumstances and, as a widow, she ends up falling in love with the young gardener when they take walks at night."

"Did she kill her husband?" Charlie asked.

Parkers eyes went wide. "I have no idea. It's not out yet. I got all that from the trailer."

Charlie nodded. "She definitely killed him."

"Hey, Miss Charlie, be careful," he shushed her with a wink. "Can't let anyone hear you theorizing like that, even if you're probably right."

"What else do I need to know?" She hoped the question would move them past the easily determined plot.

"Katherina is the more well-known of the two, and slightly older at around thirty-eight. She lives in Hollywood but also has a house in France, I think. Elliot is newer to acting and just twenty-four. He was actually discovered through a social media app and offered a small role in a movie with Harrison Ford. I guess his career grew from there."

"And they're here early because?"

Her question seemed to stump Parker. "Who knows? Stars do what they want?" He shrugged.

"I wonder if they were trying to avoid the additional publicity of coming on the day they are expected." From where she stood with Parker, she could see Felipe simpering to a tall, beautiful, blonde woman wearing a beige sheath dress and black high heels that accentuated her height. Her hair was pulled back into a severe ponytail, and her makeup was enough that Charlie could see it from across the room, though it didn't look garish.

The man next to her was occupied by his phone. He wore a loosely buttoned, light-blue shirt with dark-wash jeans. A blazer rested over his arm, and his light brown hair looked mussed as if he'd recently run a hand through it. Still, Charlie could see the classic handsomeness of his features. Sharp jawline, aquiline nose, muscled arms, and chest tapering to a narrow waist. Classically good-looking.

Behind him and next to the tall blonde woman stood a man. He divided Felipe's attention between Katherina and himself and looked as if he thought himself important. By the way Felipe deferred to him, he likely was.

"Who's the man?" she asked Parker, content to observe from the sidelines.

"That's Katherina's manager. He's made some pretty outlandish requests, and I'm sure that's all part of what they are talking about now."

"Like what?" she asked.

"Checking in a day early is one of them," Parker explained. "But also, since they will be here a week promoting the premiere next Friday, he's demanding to know what kind of security we have."

Charlie frowned. "Is she afraid for her safety?"

"It's about *the* necklace."

Charlie frowned. "What necklace?"

"Do you even own a phone?" Parker sighed, but Charlie could tell it was good-natured. "She's got a ton of jewels on loan from different places, but they come to her and, as far as I know, have their own set of safety protocols. This time, she's brought a keepsake of her grandmother's, also a well-known actress—Patrice Kent. Please tell me you've heard of her."

Charlie nodded. "In fact, I have."

"Good. Anyway, she's brought some of her grandmother's jewelry but doesn't want to keep it in the hotel safe. There's one necklace in particular she's worried about. I can't even begin to guess how much it's worth."

"Why would she bring something like that?"

"Acclaim. Notoriety. You name it. It's all over social media sites about how she'll be wearing it this week," Parker said.

As Charlie looked back to where Felipe still stood talking to both the actress and her manager, she saw the lines of tension written across his shoulders. She didn't envy him his job, but she knew he would hold fast. While the hotel was secure, their vault-like safe was far better protection than an in-room safe. She knew that from first-hand experience when a guest had claimed to use their in-room safe instead of the hotel's safe.

"Who are the other people with them?" she asked, returning her focus to the group in the middle of the lobby.

"I think the young woman with red hair is her assistant, the young man is Elliot Armstrong, that's his best friend turned manager Raji White, that's some famous makeup artist whose name I can't remember, and I don't know who the other three are."

"Quite a crew they are traveling with," Charlie commented.

"They're all part of the event that you're planning here. I know vendors trying to get them items of clothing or gifts have been stopping by non-stop as well. Not everyone is a guest."

Charlie felt exhausted just looking at them all, but she also felt like it was her chance to help Felipe. He'd been the one to offer her the job of concierge at the luxurious resort and helping him out of a sticky situation with temperamental stars was the least she could do.

"Thanks for all the intel—I mean, info—Parker."

He offered her a narrow-eyed look but nodded. "Any time, Miss Charlie."

She pulled her shoulders back, kept her head high, and adjusted the bottom of her black Pearl Sands Resort polo where it tucked into her slacks. She was a professional and, while she wasn't adept at working with Hollywood's elite, she could help the manager of the hotel with details if he needed it.

Hoping she wasn't stepping into a hornets' nest, Charlie joined the conversation as unobtrusively as possible. Her appearance in the center of the lobby gained the attention of the younger star, Elliot. He looked up from his phone and appraised her, his eyes bouncing between Felipe in his impeccable clothing and her with a staff polo.

"As I was saying, Ms. Kent, please do not fear. Our vault is extremely secure."

"But I would feel better if the items were *with* me." She turned to face her manager. "Thornton, you said you'd handled this."

"I actually suggested that you consider keeping them in the resort's vault. Mr. Delgado, certainly there's a compromise—" The manager's gaze stopped on Charlie and took on a look of disgust. "Who are you?"

Charlie felt the actress's gaze on her as well, but she held the manger's indignant look. "I'm Charlene Davis. I'm the concierge here."

"We don't need you right now." Thornton acted like he could dismiss her, and Charlie felt her ire rise.

"I was only coming over to see if I could be of assistance. Mr. Delgado?"

Curiosity shadowed Felipe's eyes, but he seemed to sense that Charlie might be able to intervene. "Ah, yes, Ms. Davis is a great asset to our resort. Not only is she our concierge, but she is also a private investigator. I wonder if you could elaborate on the safety of using the hotel vault rather than the in-room ones, Ms. Davis?"

Charlie jumped into a detailed description of the resort's vault, something she'd looked into to reassure some guests a few weeks ago, and was able to easily explain all of the features that it seemed Felipe hadn't thought to detail.

"So, you're guaranteeing that it's safer?" Katherina said. She worried her lower lip for a moment before releasing it, as if noticing what she was doing.

"Much, Ms. Kent. I can understand the desire to keep valuables with you, but in fact, it is more likely that something could happen to them there versus our secured vault."

Charlie knew the moment she'd convinced the woman, and Felipe did too. "Ms. Kent, if you will follow me, you can personally oversee their enclosure to our vault."

Katherina looked from Thornton to Felipe then cast one last glance at Charlie. She seemed to read the confidence in Charlie's look because she took a deep breath, thrust her shoulders back even further, and nodded.

"Thank you. Let's do that." Turning to the young woman behind her, she said, "Finish our check-in and get my things unpacked, Gwyn. Then call Lars. I'm going to need him after all. Thank you."

The young red-headed woman nodded once and Charlie half expected a curtsey, but instead, she grabbed a handle of each suitcase and took a few teetering steps. It was only then that Charlie noticed her four-inch tall, spike heels.

"Need a hand?" Elliot asked.

Gwyn's cheeks turned as red as her hair, but she shook her head quickly, sending her bangs into her eyes. "No. Thanks, though." She cast a glance between Elliot and his friend Raji before scurrying off as fast as her heels would let her. Charlie only hoped she wouldn't slip on the travertine tile.

"Mrs. Davis?" Elliot said.

Charlie turned her attention back to the two younger men who looked to be in their early twenties. "It's Ms. But feel free to call me Charlie."

"Charlie," Elliot said, grinning. "I like it. I'm Elliot Armstrong, and this is Raji White."

"Nice to meet you both. Can I help you with anything as you settle in to your stay?"

"Nah." His grin widened. "But I appreciated how you handled Katherina. She can be a bit...nervous sometimes."

"Understandable when you have valuables to safeguard."

His eyes narrowed. "True. Can you point us to our suite?"

"Absolutely," Charlie said. She gave them directions and watched them walk off. She noticed that Elliot carried his own bags, as did Raji.

It was clear there was a line between seasoned star and new, but what did that mean for the rest of their stay?

Only time would tell.

2

CHARLIE HAD ENDURED a busy day finalizing preparations for the next night's gala. While she'd tried her best to understand the week-long festivities centered around the new movie, *A Night of Starlight*, she couldn't completely comprehend the extravagance. A full week of activities for one movie?

They were starting the week of the premier with a "bang," as Felipe had put it. A gala to end all galas set in the South Sea Ballroom of the Pearl Sands. Along with the resort's event coordinator Margery, Charlie and Juliana had assembled an additional skeleton crew of maintenance men, a few spare groundskeepers, and some maids with a desire for overtime in order to be able to quickly transform the space into something worthy of the Gilded Age.

Gold and black had been pushed into overdrive with accents in every available area. From the place settings to the stage decorations, everything had a touch of elegance that elevated the already stunning architecture of the ballroom itself.

They had created space for three hundred guests in addition to an overly elegant table at the front of the room on a raised platform. Charlie had joked with Juliana that the stars must have really wanted people to see them eat, to which Juliana gave her a horrified look that she'd be joking about such things, but Charlie could tell she was hiding a smile.

The room was finally done, and the menu had been perfected down to the crème brûlée with gold flakes, fresh blackberries, and chocolate mint springs, which meant Charlie could relax until the next night when she would oversee the gala. Along with Margery, she would ensure things went as smoothly as they'd planned for.

Her feet ached despite her comfortable footwear, and her neck and shoulders were perpetually tight from the stress of the day, but she had all of Saturday off until the gala. She planned on taking advantage of it.

A nice, hot bath tonight, some takeout from one of her favorite restaurants, and maybe even a movie to—

Three figures stood outside of her door as she walked down the greenery-laden path to the staff cottage. She squinted until she made out who it was and sudden realization hit her.

"Crime club night!" a voice called out, raising a bottle of something over their head.

"Ramona?"

"Don't think you could get away with a *murder club* without me hearing about it and demanding entrance, do you? I mean, who do you think I am?" Ramona Munter assessed Charlie with sharp blue eyes. Her gray hair was cropped short, and she wore a loose-fitting, flowy navy top with large white flowers and cream leggings.

"I have no idea what you're talking about," Charlie said, looking behind the woman to her friends Valentina and Stephen Lopez. Valentina was the head of housekeeping at the resort and had immediately befriended Charlie during her first week on the job. Her husband Stephen had also proved to be a good friend and, while she was normally excited to see her friends, tonight she wanted nothing more than to curl up on her couch and zone out to a movie.

"I think that's our fault," Valentina said. All eyes turned to her, and Charlie noticed that she'd gotten her hip-length hair cut several inches. It was a rich, dark brown and naturally highlighted from the sun. Her tanned skin matched that of her husband's, though that was where the correlations ended.

Stephen was an English professor at a local community college and tended to dress the part without even meaning to in button-up collared shirts and pleated pants. Valentina, on the other hand, wore stylish, but business-appropriate, clothing every day. Tonight was no exception, aside from the fact the pants had been traded in for shorts and a t-shirt. Valentina showed off tanned legs and arms with her own combo of bright yellow tank-top and white shorts.

"I— I may be too tired for this conversation," Charlie admitted with a laugh. "Come on in."

"I told you we should wait until next week." Charlie heard Stephen whisper loudly to Valentina.

"She needed a break. Besides, next weekend is the premiere, so it was this weekend or not for a month since we'll be leaving for vacation after that."

Charlie was still trying to piece together what they were saying when a glorious smell reached her nose and she spun around, halfway to her bedroom where she'd intend to change into shorts and a t-shirt. "Did you bring food?"

"You bet we did," Ramona said. She held up a massive paper bag in the opposite hand from the wine bottle that Charlie could now make out to be a very expensive brand. Then again, she'd never known Ramona to do anything simply.

She'd met Ramona on her very first day at work when the woman had pretended to be an incensed customer, taking all too much glee from her undercover assignment from Felipe. It had been off-putting at first, but the woman's charm and charisma had easily won Charlie over.

Now, whenever Ramona stayed at the resort, which was frequently, the two always found time for coffee or a meal to catch up.

"I'll be right out," Charlie said. "Don't make me wait on food."

She disappeared into her room and replayed what Ramona had said. Crime club?

Deciding that reasoning out what the woman was saying wasn't worth the time it would take when she could ask her outright in the next few minutes, Charlie changed quickly and stooped by the thermostat on her way back to the main room to turn the air conditioner a few degrees cooler.

Despite having lived in Florida for years now, Charlie—born and bred in New York City—hadn't fully adjusted to the humidity that accompanied a Floridian August heatwave.

"This looks good. Lucio's?" Charlie said, reaching for a plate that Ramona had just finished spooning pasta into.

"Hey, that was mine." She grinned at Charlie.

"Thanks," was all Charlie said.

The woman laughed and went back to spoon her own portion before taking a moment to pour four glasses of chilled white wine. "Yes. Their pasta alfredo with bay shrimp is my absolute obsession."

Charlie hid her smile at the woman's dramatic flair and settled into her newly acquired lounge chair complete with opening footrest while Ramona took the floor—something she always did—and Valentina and Stephen shared the couch.

"Now, tell me what I signed up for but didn't remember?" Charlie twirled a forkful of the fettucine and enjoyed her first bite of the cheesy deliciousness.

"Crime club." Ramona said it so matter-of-factly that Charlie began to wonder if she really had agreed to something and completely forgotten about it.

"To be fair, that was *your* name for it," Valentina addressed Ramona.

"I advocated for book club," Stephen said, getting his two cents in.

His statement took Charlie back to her past post in Key West. She'd been an investigator for Cutlass Investigations, working for a hardnosed but brilliant man named Doug Thacker who had pushed Charlie to her limits, but in the best way.

There, in a boutique bed-and-breakfast, one of his clients-turned-investigator had a successful book club she'd hosted. Charlie had heard Doug talk about it in the past and how he thought it was hilarious how they'd all banded together on several occasions to solve crimes.

At the time, Charlie had thought the idea of a book club silly, but hearing Stephen say it and realizing her own, new-found sense of connection so different from her past, Charlie almost said she'd consider a book club. *Almost.*

"The idea," Ramona began, "was to give us true crime addicts a little something fun to distract ourselves with."

"You like true crime?" Charlie said, turning back into the conversation.

"Yes." Ramona looked affronted, as if Charlie should know everything about her despite the short duration of their friendship.

"Good to know," was all Charlie said. She forked another mouthful of pasta, savoring the tang of the cheese and the subtle flavor of the shrimp.

"So here we are. The first meeting of the Pearl Sands Crime Club." Ramona held her hands out as if to say *ta-da*.

"I don't get it," Charlie said. She looked from Ramona to Stephen and Valentina. "What do we do?"

"Talk about crime, I guess," Stephen said, his dry humor making Charlie grin.

"No one knows what this is about?" Charlie turned back to Ramona. "Did you come up with this today?"

She looked guilty. "Maybe."

"Ramona, if you wanted to get together, all you had to do was ask." Charlie took a sip of the white wine. It ran extra cold down her throat but left a pleasant burning sensation. She wasn't one to drink much, but the feeling was relaxing after such a long and busy day.

"I don't want to just *get together*," Ramona said, "I want to have a purpose. A club. Everyone has their nice charcuterie book clubs, but I wanted us to have a real-life murder club."

"Crime club," Valentina amended. "The other way makes it sound like we're planning something."

Charlie almost laughed at Valentina's horrified look, but she had to agree. "I suppose we could watch an episode of some documentary or something. Would that give you the purpose you're looking for, Ramona?"

"I'd be okay with that," Stephen added.

"Of course you would. You do that every night anyway." Valentina laughed, shaking her head.

"And you're right there with me." He winked.

Ramona considered this and nodded slowly. "I suppose it could work."

"Good. Now, can I be honest and say tonight is not the best night to start this club of ours?" Charlie stifled a yawn. "Today was grueling and, as much as I'd love to put on something to watch, I don't think I'd make it past the introduction."

Her friends nodded in understanding and finished their pasta as they chatted about the upcoming week of events. Charlie was thankful for the company but, admittedly, even more thankful when they said good night and she could shower and topple into bed.

As she picked up the true crime novel from the bedside table, she laughed. She had never been a person to be in a club, but here she was, Charlene Davis, member of the Pearl Sands Crime Club. Wonders would never cease.

CHARLIE SLOWED her pace as the Pearl Sands Resort came into view. Her heart pounded from running on the beach, and she moved closer to the water where the sand was more firmly packed.

She might be nearing sixty, but she still made the effort to get out and run on the beach at least three times a week. Then again, 'run' was a gracious word for her plodding pace, but she didn't mind. It was the movement that mattered. Besides, she *felt* good.

That, and the sea spray that gusted around from the ebb and flow of the waves invigorated her. It pushed her to keep going.

The resort loomed ahead, but Charlie slowed even more. She had woken up earlier than her body would have liked, but her mind was awake and buzzing despite the fact it was her day off. That was the beauty of expanding her department, no matter that the expansion was just one person. Baby steps would get her to a place where there were enough employees that everyone would get at least one weekend off a month. Perhaps more.

A particularly enthusiastic wave rushed toward her and she barely managed to jump out of the way before it soaked through her tennis shoes. Laughing to herself, she almost didn't see the man running along the beach toward her.

His long-legged strides were at once recognizable, and the familiar spiking of her pulse had nothing to do with her run this time.

Nelson Hall, potter and former military Criminal Investigation Division officer, came jogging toward her, a grin on his tanned and handsome features. His dark brown hair showed heavy patches of gray at his temples and streaked throughout, but his beard still remained mostly dark. She was surprised to see it so full and wondered when she'd seen him last.

"Good morning," he said, coming to a stop in front of her. She noticed how easily he caught his breath and tried not to be too jealous. His military training had taught him well, but it was clear Nelson kept up with his own healthy routine with how in shape he was.

"Morning. Perfect day for a run," she commented, kicking up a leg to stretch her sore quad muscles.

"You almost got caught by that wave." His grin widened, showing perfectly straight, white teeth.

"I saw it coming in plenty of time."

"Sure." He grinned and lunged into his own stretch.

They both faced the water, not willing to be caught unaware again, and Charlie thought of the last real conversation they'd had. It had been at an art gallery opening, and she'd said some things she wished she hadn't.

By the time her stubborn nature had calmed somewhat, Nelson was working sixteen-hour days to refill his pottery shop, *Ceramica*, with new items since most of his inventory had been smashed by a burglar.

Every time she'd gone to make amends with him, it never felt right. Perhaps some of that was due to her stubbornness, but part of her thought he owed her an apology as well. In reality, the conversation she'd had with the new detective on the force, Sophia Perez, had opened Charlie's eyes to truths about Nelson's history that she'd hoped he would have shared with her. Perhaps that was the real block between them.

Then again, he'd accused her of keeping her past a secret, and she couldn't argue that. It seemed there were things in both of their pasts that they wished would be left there, but Charlie wasn't sure she could continue the friendship without knowing more about Nelson as it seemed to directly affect their present. She wondered if he felt the same way about her.

"Are you doing most of the planning for the events this week?" he asked, breaking into her thoughts.

"Some, yes, but in tandem with the event coordinator. Juliana and I are mostly in charge of the gala tomorrow night, though that is good to go at this point. I'm a little nervous about the premiere, though. We almost double-booked, which meant that one showing had to move to the night before, which gives us a day to set up everything." Charlie's chest tightened at the mere thought.

"But with my ramshackle team, we'll get it done." She laughed and turned to find Nelson's gaze on her.

"I've missed you, Charlie."

So many emotions flooded through her. Warmth at his words and the intent look he gave her vied for attention despite the other, darker thoughts that hurt to even acknowledge. Like the fact that she hadn't stopped him from coming to see her. He'd done that on his own.

"There is a lot going on behind those eyes," he said, "and I think some of that is my fault."

Surprise raised her eyebrows. "Maybe not just you."

His half-smile helped her relax enough to ask, "How is the shop coming along?"

His expression darkened, but she knew it wasn't because of her.

"They broke so much good pottery." His fists clenched at his sides before she watched him consciously relax them. "But I'm making progress. I'm hoping for a soft reopening in a few weeks."

"I'm glad to hear that. And I'm sorry—again."

"It wasn't your fault. There was no real connection to the class, thankfully."

He spoke of the pottery class she'd offered to their guests as the first of what she hoped to be many interactive activities that resort guests could sign up for. It had ended rather disastrously though, and Felipe had put a hold on further classes—at least for the moment.

"Still…" She held her hands up. "I feel somewhat responsible."

"Don't." His smile relaxed into a genuine one. "Want to go get some coffee?"

She opened her mouth to agree but closed it again. Since their tiff at the art gallery, Charlie had been spending more time with Felipe. While she was careful not to accept all of his invitations, she had enjoyed the time they were spending together and realized that, from Felipe's perspective, his companionship might be more than just friendship. She wondered how he would feel about her going to coffee with Nelson. Then again, they had no agreement and it had been weeks since they'd gone out— his time needing to be spent with his mother.

In that space, she'd come to consider their time together as fun and lighthearted, but nothing more—at least not on her end.

Nelson's invitation drew her to say yes. He had been among the first to welcome her to the Pearl Sands Resort, and she'd enjoyed his easygoing nature and quick, intelligent mind. She wanted to say yes, but needing to settle things with Felipe held her back.

"Not this time. I've promised myself not to commit to anything today." She flashed a smile. "But perhaps in the future."

He returned the smile, and she searched for any hint that she'd offended him but couldn't find any. "Sounds good. Enjoy your day off."

Without another word, he took off down the beach in the opposite direction, toward the small residential end of the tied island the Pearl Sands Resort sat on. While she didn't know where exactly, she knew Nelson did have a house down there. This week wouldn't allow for extra time for her, or Felipe for that matter, but she'd make it a priority to figure out where they stood. Best to keep their working relationship just that.

Charlie picked up her pace to a brisk walk and made it back to her cottage in good time. Her stomach growled, and she made a beeline for the coffee maker before popping in a piece of toast and putting a skillet on to fry an egg.

She'd just finished wiping up the rest of the runny yoke with her toast when a knock sounded on her door. Hoping it wasn't someone asking her to help with something she'd forgotten, Charlie opened the door to find Detective Sophia Perez sanding there, two cups of coffee in hand.

"Don't worry, I'm not going to make this a habit." The woman, shorter than Charlie by a few inches, brushed past her without an invite and set the coffee on the table between them.

Sophia wore her dark brown hair pulled back in a low bun, reminiscent of how she wore it when in uniform, but today, she had on jean shorts and a worn dark-blue t-shirt with a police academy logo on it.

Charlie took a seat and stared back at the woman. "Well, want to tell me why you're here then? Or do you want to make me guess?"

The smallest hint of a smile tugged at the detective's lips. "I know we haven't known each other long, but I stand by my reassessment of you. You're good people."

Charlie took a sip of the coffee and enjoyed the bold flavor. She knew Sophia's husband had made it as it was her second time trying the delicious brew. She also knew that Sophia was talking about their last conversation months before. The one where she'd opened up to Charlie, capitulating that she'd been biased upon their first meeting. She'd also shared that Nelson had been married to her sister before the woman died.

"Thank you, I think."

"You know I judged you wrongly at first, and I'm not going to apologize again for that." She winked and took a sip of her coffee. "But I'm here on less-than-official business, so I might as well get to it."

This had Charlie sitting up straighter. She had a feeling the woman had clarified her presence because she was going to share something she wasn't necessarily authorized to, but she was going to do it anyway. "Consider me intrigued."

"I know you're in charge of some of the activities that are coming up at the resort." Charlie wanted to ask *how* she knew that but knew it was a waste of time, so she remained silent. "While we'll have an elevated police presence here, I'm afraid that someone might take advantage of the chaos."

"In what way?" Charlie asked.

"Theft." Sophia spat the word out. "I've been investigating a string of robberies—essentially cat burglaries—in the area and have come to realize there is something off about them."

Charlie leaned forward, elbow on the table. "Wrong how?"

"Too good. Too precise. They were able to get into homes that should have been impenetrable."

"Have you checked with the cleaning staff? Gardeners? Recent maintenance done on the properties?"

Sophia grinned. "You've clearly done this a time or two."

Charlie shrugged. "It was my life for a long time."

A memory came back to her of a specific string of robberies and how she'd done stakeout after stakeout until it finally paid off. The rush when she'd captured the burglar in action and handed him over to the police was like nothing else she'd ever felt. She almost missed it— then again, perhaps it was more than 'almost.'

"To answer your questions, yes, we've checked and re-checked all of those avenues. No one was seen despite there being cameras. Not one piece of furniture is out of place nor has there been forced entry. No evidence left behind—well, almost."

"What do you mean, 'almost'?"

"There was a partial fingerprint, but that's all we've found. It didn't line up to anyone in the system. It's like they are a ghost walking through walls, though I know that's not possible."

"And you're afraid they'll shift their target to the guests of the Pearl Sands? That seems illogical. I mean, it's one thing for a burglar to be good at house jobs or what have you, but it's another to switch to a resort like this with cameras everywhere and security at its max."

"I agree. It's more of a…" She trailed off and wrinkled her nose. "A gut feeling, I guess."

"Okay." Charlie's tone must have portrayed how skeptical she was.

"I know. I don't usually rely on that, but I know we all have it. That instinct that tells us something is off. The timing of these robberies is what I think bothers me the most."

"When did they start?"

"A week after the announcement that the Pearl Sands was the location of the premiere—which, as you know, was done late on purpose."

Charlie did know what she meant. They had already known the premiere was coming for months before it was announced to the public. It had been done on purpose to avoid causing too much chaos. Whoever was coming already had reservations by that point.

"Have any been in close proximity?"

Sophia shrugged. "You could say they all are since they are within a five-mile radius of the Pearl Sands, but if you mean the northern area of Barnabe Island, then no. Not yet, at least."

Charlie nodded. "So you're here to what? Warn me?"

"In a way. I know you're not on security and, while I will be involving them of course, I wanted one other pair of eyes out."

"Of course." Charlie allowed a small smile. "But answer me this: why are *you* on this case?"

Sophia rolled her eyes at Charlie's blunt question, but it was a good one. The detective was with homicide, so burglary seemed out of her territory.

"I guess you could say I got the short straw. The woman working home invasions is a friend and she's finishing up her final month of maternity leave. She requested I take her caseload when possible, and my boss agreed."

"Fun. Thanks for cluing me in." Charlie took another sip of the excellent coffee and grinned. "You know, I think we could actually be friends one day."

Sophia let out a bark of a laugh. "Don't go all soft on me."

"I wouldn't dream of it."

3

GLITZ AND GLAMOUR covered every surface. Charlie was overwhelmed by the sheer weight of the wealth that surrounded her. Having grown up the only child of a New York cop, she had never known a life of opulence, but after moving to Key West, she'd seen it from afar. Beautiful houses, expensive clothing, fancy boats. It had been overwhelming at first, but she'd grown somewhat accustomed to it.

While it still felt far-off, she was much closer to it now that she was working at the Pearl Sands. She'd thought months of being surrounded by affluent guests and learning to cater to their every whim would have prepared her for the night, but that was far from the truth. This was one level up in every way.

In the style of a true Hollywood event, a red carpet had been laid out to receive the guests from the many limos that would convey them to the resort. The lobby had been closed off to guests for the night and transitioned to an elegant entrance that led the way to the grand ballroom where the opening night gala was to take place.

Charlie checked the straps of her borrowed black designer dress. It had sleek lines that hugged her slight curves and dropped to just below her knee. The back dipped low but black lace filled the empty space between the straps—the very ones that seemed to want to slip off her shoulders. Her heels were lower than was appropriate for the night, but that was necessary with the amount of walking she would need to do.

"You look stunning," Valerie said. She wore a floor-length, burgundy silk gown that, accompanied by her stunning beauty, made her look like an actress herself. "I'm so glad I could find a dress that fit you."

Charlie laughed. "I have never worn something so nice before."

"Work here long enough and we'll get you a full wardrobe. I'm still surprised you didn't want to buy a dress for this. It'll come in handy."

While Charlie knew that Valentina had been at the resort for years and worked her way up to head of housekeeping, she wasn't in the same position as her friend. Her wage was generous and she had savings set aside, but Charlie hadn't felt in a place to spend hundreds on a dress when her friend had a whole spare closet she could borrow from. She kept those thoughts to herself lest she been seen as cheap, though she knew her friend would never judge her in that way.

Instead she said, "Maybe one day."

Valentina shrugged. She'd volunteered to help oversee the waitstaff along with another head of staff, and Charlie knew she loved dressing the part.

They turned as the first limo arrived. Paparazzi surged *en mass* and soon the entrance was flooded with flashes and shouts for poses and comments. Charlie watched, dazed, as a beautiful young woman took the arm of her escort and walked the length of the carpet toward the lobby doors. Her gold gown sparkled in the camera flashes, and she walked confidently despite the height of her heels.

"That's Amelia Von Hart. She was in that action film with that one actor…" Valentina looked up in thought. "I can't remember his name."

"Don't bother," Charlie laughed. "I wouldn't know who he was anyway."

"You're no fun. Who will I gawk with over all these stars?" Valentina winked at Charlie, who merely shrugged.

"No gawking here, but I do have a few details to check on. Talk to you later?"

Valentina nodded, and Charlie stepped past and through the lobby doors. While the space was usually elegant and overwhelmingly chic, tonight there were vases upon vases of red roses interspersed with gold-dipped roses. Twists of black glass made by a local artisan shot up from the center of each gold vase and mirrored the table settings that Charlie and Margery had chosen.

Charlie was pleased with the details and thought they evoked a properly elegant feeling while refraining from being over-the-top. As she passed them, she double-checked that the flowers weren't wilting. She'd tasked one of the front desk assistants to water them earlier that day, and it looked as if they'd held up their end of the bargain.

Heels clacking on the marble floor, Charlie took the passthrough to the grand ballroom, skirting other couples as they took their time admiring the artwork and resort's beauty. Live music reached her before she even reached the doors, and she caught hints of laughter as it floated through the open doors.

Two attendants stood at the doors dressed in resort-issued suits and nodded at her as she stepped inside. There was a surprising number of guests staying at the resort for the week, and she saw that most of them had already arrived even as a steady stream of guests began pouring in through the lobby entrance as well.

At the front of the ballroom, a five-piece jazz ensemble played classic tunes. As the night wore on, they would switch to covers of more modern songs, but she'd insisted they stay as background music to start off the night. It lent the perfect atmosphere to the room, which smelled faintly of roses and that night's dinner.

Next to the band was the main stage where the speeches and keynote would be held, and on the opposite side from the band was the raised platform where the cast of *A Night of Starlight* would sit. She had no idea why it was desirable for the attendees of the gala to watch the cast eat their five-hundred-a-plate dinner, but hers was not to question, only to organize.

"You have done an excellent job with this." Felipe appeared at her elbow and startled her. She'd been so engrossed checking on everything that she hadn't even heard him come up next to her.

"Thank you. Margery and I had an amazing crew helping me."

"Ah yes, but it was your vision, was it not?" He quirked an eyebrow at her, which made her smile. "Margery told me you took to the event planning better than she had hoped."

Charlie laughed. "Perhaps, but it was out of necessity since she couldn't be here tonight. Besides, Juliana also helped quite a bit with all of this."

"She has been a good choice for promotion to her new position. Thank you for that recommendation."

"And thank you for taking my recommendation."

Her looked down at her, the black of his tuxedo contrasting pleasantly with his deeply tanned skin. His dark brown eyes reflected the glowing lights, and she saw something in his look that made her stomach clench. It reminded her that they needed to have a discussion.

"Did you think I would not?"

It took Charlie a second to remember what she had said before. "It's not that. It's just that there are a hundred people who could have qualified for the position, but you asked my opinion."

"As I will continue to do." He dipped his head. "I do need to attend to a few things but allow me to say that you look positively stunning tonight."

Charlie knew her cheeks had flushed at his compliment, but all she did was smile and nod. He had the decency not to address the blush and dipped his head once before he walked off to the other end of the room. If Felipe was anything, he was always a gentleman.

Swallowing, Charlie moved toward the kitchen. She mentally went through the list she and Margery had come up with regarding the night. The event coordinator had been heart-sick she'd miss the premiere week, but she'd planned her twenty-year anniversary trip long before they'd known about the premiere.

The change had thrust Charlie into a role she hadn't been planning on—coordinating events, decorating, and Margery's team—but she'd enjoyed it more than she thought she would. Not that she wanted to change jobs. She was more than happy coordinating guests' excursions and helping them find the perfect place for dinner over having to organizing the details for hundreds of guests at once.

Once in the controlled chaos of the bustling kitchen, she conferred with the head chef, though only briefly as he had a kitchen of chefs to oversee. She confirmed that everything was on schedule and ready, then she returned to the main gala.

The night would begin fifteen minutes late, per the event host who, with her team, had prepared everything that didn't pertain to the resort location itself. They had speeches lined up, a keynote speaker, and space for the lead actors to say a few words.

Then dessert would be served and the dance floor, and open bar, would be opened for the guests. Charlie had a feeling that things might get rowdy, but that was where Ben Simmons came in. As head of security for the resort, he would be in charge of keeping the peace for the attendees of the gala as well as for the resort guests. It was a job Charlie didn't envy.

She saw Ben at the back of the grand ballroom but hesitated to check in with him. They hadn't seen eye-to-eye since Felipe had asked her to investigate a case that had occurred on resort property while Ben was away on vacation. Their mild rivalry had only continued as Felipe had asked her—yet again—to look into another incident months later.

Ben had gone out of his way to undermine her with the police but, in the end, it had worked itself out. That didn't mean that their communication had been easy since then. He'd treated her with minor disdain ever since, but she knew there was no point in trying to change his mind. He would have to come to that on his own.

Rather than chance a confrontation at the gala, which she doubted would happen but didn't want to take the risk, Charlie checked in with his second-in-command, who stood on the opposite side of the ballroom. When he gave the affirmative that everything was in order, Charlie finally let herself relax some.

Perhaps tonight really would go off without problems. Or was that too much to ask?

CHARLIE STIFLED a yawn and blinked rapidly. She'd managed to make it through two hours of the gala so far, but it was getting late and she was beat. Perhaps she should have tried to get in more sleep before the start of the week, knowing it was going to be one of her busiest so far at the Pearl Sands, but there hadn't been time to sleep in.

A new speaker took the stage. Charlie prepared herself for another half-hour speech, but the man was brief. With a flourish, he called up Katherina Kent and Elliot Armstrong, the leads of the movie premiering.

Katherina wore a stunning gown of deep plum silk that hugged curves any woman would be jealous of. Her silver heels looked as if they were made of diamonds and caught the light at every movement as she climbed the stairs to the stage. The dress's thigh-high slit opened to reveal shapely legs at every step, and Charlie saw many men in the front row admiring the view.

With a quick roll of her eyes, Charlie shifted her gaze to the young man with the starlet. He was handsome in the way young surfers were. Blond hair swooped back from his forehead in a way that made it look effortless, though it was likely anything but. His broad shoulders pulled taut the green velvet fabric of his jacket, which was worn over a brilliant white shirt and no tie. As he ascended the steps, she caught sight of almost too-short pants that gave a clear view of his bare ankles in expensive shoes.

Stars. They did everything impractically, or so she thought. It had to be uncomfortable to wear dress shoes without socks or a dress with a slit that threatened to expose enough to give the tabloids a story. Then again, that was a world they lived in and she did not.

As Katherina stopped next to the podium and the man who had announced them, Charlie finally got a good view of the woman's jewelry. If rumors could be believed, the ensemble was worth over a million dollars, and she had even *more* gems in the hotel vault. Her necklace and earrings sparkled in the brilliant stage lighting, and Charlie caught sight of a diamond bracelet as well.

Charlie couldn't even begin to guess what it felt like to wear something worth so much. Not to mention the fact it wasn't even *hers*. Some jeweler had loaned it to her to wear in hopes that the name recognition of the star would bring them business. It was a risk Charlie couldn't begin to calculate, but it must have been a successful tactic since the risk had been taken.

The announcer stepped forward and, while looking back at the stars, began to speak. "We are so pleased to recognize such talent before you all tonight."

Applause interrupted his words, and Charlie looked out over the rows of circular tables. Everyone was enraptured, eyes on the stage and the massive screen above that gave an up-close view of the speaker. She hadn't caught his name.

"Tonight kicks off a week-long celebration of *A Night of Starlight*, but I wanted you to hear a few words from our stars first. Elliot, why don't we start with you as the newcomer to the Hollywood scene."

Charlie couldn't be certain, but Elliot's smile appeared forced as he stood at the podium. He pulled a stack of what looked like notecards from his pocket and glanced down at them.

"It's an honor to be here tonight." More applause thundered around the room. "And a bit of a dream come true. I mean, do you see who I'm standing next to?"

The crowd laughed with him as he made a show of looking at Katherina and then turning back to the audience as if to say, *I know, I can't believe it either.*

"I've had many dreams in my life, and I was sure most of them would *not* come true, but being in a movie with such talented actors, and bringing something like *A Night of Starlight* to fruition, has been beyond my wildest dreams. Thank you for supporting us in this venture. We hope you love it." He placed his hands together and made a quick bow before he stepped back to give Katherina the stage.

Charlie had to give the young man credit. He'd spoken well, not said too much, and acted in a deferential manner that respected Katherina as a more experienced actor but also a co-star. Elliot might be young, but he was doing all the right things to succeed—if Charlie had to guess.

Katherina stepped up to the mic and picked up her own cards that seemed to have been left their earlier since Charlie knew there had been nothing in her hands and no way her dress had pockets. Charlie was fairly certain Elliot hadn't actually used his cue cards, but she wondered if the stars were required to say specific things and they didn't want to forget them.

"I echo what my co-star said. We are so grateful to be here and hope that what we've made will be equally as inspiring as it is enchanting."

Charlie tuned out some as the star went on to dive into the depths of how she'd gotten the script. It was clear from the differing lengths of their speeches who was the seasoned actor and who was new to the scene.

The table in front of Charlie dissolved into whispered conversation, and Charlie took note of how most guests did the same as Katherina continued. It wasn't boring, per se, but Charlie wondered about the dessert she'd seen back in the kitchen. If she was thinking about it, she was certain the guests were as well.

Charlie had just decided to make her way around the room to see how the plans for serving dessert after this speech were progressing when the air of the room shifted. The whispered conversations grew more insistent, and Charlie noticed that Katherina had stopped speaking.

There, illuminated by the jumbo screen, Katherina's face had gone pale—more so than just the effects of her makeup—and the card held with both hands shook so violently that Charlie thought the woman could be having a health emergency.

Then, Katherina's eyes snapped up. "Who did this?" She held up the card and waved it around, though all that could be seen were angry red letters.

Charlie acted without thought and raced to the stage, beating the security team as the audience burst into shocked conversation.

"Who!" Katherina said, her words echoing through the space as both Elliot and the speaker tried to calm her down with magnified whispers.

"Calm down, Kat," Elliot said.

"I'm sure it's just a joke," the announcer said.

Charlie looked up to the sound booth and made a slash across her throat. The sound and the enlarged picture cut off just as Charlie made it to the podium.

In that moment, she was thankful for the borrowed dress. It was an odd thing to think of, but she could just imagine how she would have looked wearing her inexpensive slacks and black t-shirt.

"Excuse me, but I'm with the Pearl Sands Resort, can I be of assistance?" Charlie asked.

"Who had access to these?" Katherina asked, her eyes blazing with fury.

Charlie looked down at the notes. It looked as if the original typed notes had been written over with a red pen. It looked as if each card held a word, but all Charlie could see was the word 'get'.

"I—I'm not sure. Do you know who was supposed to put them here?"

"I—" Katherina closed her mouth and shrugged. "I actually don't know."

While Charlie could tell the woman was still furious, she seemed to be calming down quickly.

"My assistant will know. Gwyn? Where is Gwyn?" Katherina looked around as if Gwyn would be right there.

"Why don't we take this off the stage?" the announcer suggested.

Charlie agreed. Before she could step back and let hotel security take over, however, Katherina grabbed her hand and began dragging her down the stairs.

"Um, I can get the head of security to help you—"

"No. I want you. You were the first to come up, and I respect someone who is quick to act. Come."

Charlie followed, feeling a little out of her element as she joined a group of people at the bottom of the stairs. A young waif of a girl rushed up to Katherina with a wide-eyed expression. She had beautiful red hair and deep green eyes with just the right touch of freckles across her nose and cheeks. Charlie thought she recognized her from the lobby when Katherina had checked in.

A tall, distinguished-looking man appeared behind her. Charlie recognized him as the man Parker had said was Katherina's manager. There were several others there as well, but Charlie hadn't seen them before.

"What's going on?" the young woman asked.

"Gwyn, who was supposed to put my notes there? Was it you?" Katherina's words held an edge.

"I— What? Your notes?" Gwyn blinked. "I gave them to someone on staff here."

Katherina turned to Charlie. "Do you know who that would be?"

Charlie squared her shoulders. She had a feeling the movie star would respect a direct approach. "This room has only been open to those setting up the event. Our security staff has kept a close eye on it as well. If a staff member was supposed to put them on the podium, I'm sure they did, and I can find out who." Charlie turned to

Gwyn. "Do you remember the name of the staff person or what they looked like?"

"Um, maybe?"

"You either do or you don't," Katherina snapped.

Gwyn blinked. "His name was Zeek, I think? I didn't get a last name. He was as tall as Mr. Blackwell but younger, like maybe mid-twenties. And he had blonde hair. That's all I remember."

While Charlie didn't know all of the staff members at the resort, it was nearly impossible with the number of staff needed to keep the resort running smoothly, she knew the man's name didn't sound familiar. "I'll look into it," she said.

"Good. Where is Felipe?" Katherina asked.

Charlie remembered how at ease the woman had been with the resort manager. It was either a benefit from her status as a star or perhaps a personal connection. Charlie's gaze scanned the room and saw him only a few tables away.

"He's coming." She flashed a look at the manager and caught the distress in his wrinkled forehead.

"I'll go up and announce the dancing," the speaker said.

Charlie still hadn't caught his name, but Katherina turned to him and flashed a grateful smile. "Thank you, Hal. I appreciate it."

He left them just as Felipe arrived. "What has happened?" He looked first to Katherina and then to Charlie.

Charlie knew her place here. Katherina had asked for her to join them, but ultimately, it was Felipe's choice as to how they would proceed.

"It's horrid," Katherina said just as the speaker—Hal—announced it was time for dessert and dancing.

Charlie half-listened as he explained that there had been a mix-up but everything was fine and now it was time to enjoy the rest of their night. She tuned back to Felipe saying, "We will do everything we can. Perhaps for now, it is best for you to return your jewelry to the vault."

"Do you think that is wise? Should I switch to another hotel?" Katherina placed a protective hand over her necklace.

Charlie saw fear in her eyes and realized whatever had been on the cards had something to do with her jewelry.

"I do not think that is necessary." Felipe flashed a forced but confident smile. "We'll call the police in to check out the threat, I promise."

Now Charlie knew she'd missed something. Was it not about the necklace but about the woman? "Threat?"

Felipe and Katherina turned to her. Without a word, the star handed over her notecards. Charlie took them and moved to a cocktail table. As she laid out the cards, it was clear to see what had bothered the actress. And threat was just the beginning.

4

"I'll get you and your pretty necklace, too." Detective Sophia Perez shook her head. "How original."

Charlie sat with the detective at a small table in one of the resort's restaurants the morning after the gala. They each had a cup of coffee and a pastry to enjoy during their quick meeting—the one that Felipe had insisted Charlie take with the detective. Also, the very same one she hadn't told Felipe she'd already arranged.

He was insistent that she look into this case and had told her in no uncertain terms at the end of the gala that she had to find a way to alleviate Katherina's worries. Charlie knew better than to assume she could, let alone would have time to, and there was the reality that this was Sophia's case.

"I mean, as threats go, it's not that...threatening." Charlie studied the color-printed photocopies of the notecards.

Katherina's speech was typed out behind the angry red words. The originals had already been sent to the lab with Katherina and Gwyn's set of prints on file for elimination. Charlie wasn't hopeful that they'd really get anything solid from the cards, but she knew it was the next step.

"It isn't, but it did its job. It startled her. You say you looked into the staff list and there is no Zeek on record?"

"I had them send over the files to your email, but no, no one by that name or any name that could reasonably be shortened to that. Then again, Gwyn, Katherina's assistant, did seem like she wasn't positive about the guy."

"But she came up with a name?" Sophia's skeptical look mirrored Charlie's own.

"After Katherina all but forced her to give us a description."

"I see." Sophia looked back at the notes. "Despite the ridiculous saying, it also feels odd to have the threat be delivered so publicly. I assume that was purposeful, but why warn us if the threat is really about burglary?"

Charlie thought about it. "It would put resort security on high alert. It would also alert the police." She gestured to the woman across from her. "And it could fluster Katherina."

"Was that the goal?" Sophia asked the question out loud, but Charlie got the feeling she was really asking herself.

"There's something else a warning like this would do." Sophia looked over at Charlie. "It would up the ante if a thief were able to make off with the necklace."

"You think this is about notoriety?"

"I'm not sure." Charlie tapped her index finger on the table. "You did mention that string of cat burglaries and that you were worried they might target the Pearl Sands next due to the sudden influx of high-profile guests because of premiere week."

"Yes, but there weren't any notes left behind in these robberies. Just a bold thief who hadn't made any mistakes yet."

"Is it possible this is connected?"

"That's a leap. I mean, the whole point of a cat burglar is stealth. This is the opposite of that." Sophia took a sip of her coffee and wrinkled her nose. "Not as good as Arturo's."

"Your husband?"

"Yes." Sophia's smile was uncharacteristically soft for a moment before she refocused on Charlie. "I don't think it matters either way if this is related to the string of burglaries or not. It just means more security and keeping an extra eye on Ms. Kent and her jewelry."

"I suppose you're right. I do think the reasoning behind *why* they alerted us to a possible threat is important, but I don't know that it changes things."

Sophia shrugged and pulled out her phone. "I'm getting heat from the higherups to ensure that Ms. Kent is happy."

Charlie could tell from the way Sophia said it that she wasn't happy catering to a star, no matter who they were, but she would do her job.

"What about you?" Sophia suddenly turned her inquisitive, dark brown eyes on Charlie.

"What about me? I'm the concierge, remember?"

Sophia made a *phhhft* sound. "And a private investigator with a rather impressive track record."

"I'm not sure if I should feel honored or offended that you checked into my background." Charlie lightened her words with a grin.

"Feel impressed. Your former employer was loath to speak about you to some unknown cop, but I finally got him to spill."

Charlie could imagine her former boss, Doug Thacker of Cutlass Investigations, treating the detective's questions with malice. "He's not an easy guy to get things out of. Like a vault, that one."

"Let's just say it was enough to back up what I already had decided about you. So, what will you do about this threat?"

Charlie sat back. The investigations she'd gotten into at the resort were the result of Felipe interfering on her behalf. She hadn't sought them out so much as given in when he'd asked. But this was different. There was no specific threat aside from the star's expensive necklace, and that was in the vault. What more could she do?

"Protection will be left to Ben."

"And investigation?" Sophia prompted.

"Will be done by the police." Charlie pointed at the woman across the table from her.

"You know the extent to which I can investigative this. There has been no crime, only the threat of one. I'm going to take it seriously, but what more do I have to go on?"

"What more would I have?" Charlie countered.

"You're here. I'm not." Sophia tipped the last of her coffee up and back then gently set the ceramic mug on the white linen tablecloth. "I'm not saying get in the way, but I am saying keep your eyes open. As any good PI would."

Charlie thought about her response before she gave it. This would already be a busy week for her and her team— especially Juliana—and she didn't want to put too much responsibility on the woman's shoulders as it was still very new for her. But could Charlie sit by and not look into what was going on with the threat given to the star?

Sophia had a good point. Security at the resort would be focused on prevention, not investigation, and Charlie would be around whereas Sophia would only be involved to the extent that she had reason to be—clues or more threats or otherwise.

DANIELLE COLLINS & MILLIE BRIGGS

There wasn't much Charlie thought she could do, but there was one thing that had caught her attention. One thread she wanted to pull.

"I'll look into it, but with the knowledge that whatever I find, you'll have to act on. My real job is going to keep me too busy for much more than that."

Sophia quirked an eyebrow. "It's too easy."

"What?" Charlie asked.

"Getting you to help me." The detective laughed and popped the last of her pastry into her mouth. She flicked a few crumbs off her fingers and stood. "Call me when you have something."

With that, Charlie watched the detective saunter out of the restaurant. She felt a little like she'd just been played.

Then again, that thread dangled in front of her and coaxed her forward, deeper into the case.

CHARLIE FOUND Gwyn lounging at the pool in a black-and-pink polka dot bikini. She had a fruity drink an arm's length away and wore a large-brimmed hat with sunglasses. She looked like she'd stepped from the pages of a magazine from the nineteen-fifties, though the cut of her suit was not quite so vintage.

"Excuse me, Miss Milford?" Charlie had looked up the woman's full name before deciding to approach her.

Gwyn languidly pulled down the sunglasses and turned an inquisitive gaze to Charlie. "Yes?"

It was obvious that she had no memory of talking with Charlie the night before. It was almost amusing the way some people lacked the basic skills of perception. Charlie chided herself for being too harsh, even if it was in her thoughts, toward the young woman.

"My name is Charlie, and I work here at the Pearl Sands." She thought that part was obvious seeing as she wore a black polo with the resort's logo on it. "We met at the gala."

The woman's freckled nose scrunched in thought, but she turned a blank stare back to Charlie. "I'm afraid I don't remember you."

Charlie almost mentioned the incredible dress she'd been wearing, positive the young woman—who was clearly concerned with fashion as her outfit and the magazines next to her drink proclaimed—would remember it, but she tried a different approach instead.

"I helped Ms. Kent after the…incident."

Gwyn's eyes went wide, and she slid her legs to the side of the chaise lounge. "Yes, now I remember you. Is something wrong?"

Charlie motioned to the seat next to her. "Would you mind if I sat for a moment?"

"Not at all." Gwyn took a sip of her drink.

"I know it was quite an eventful night and things were so chaotic, but I wanted to ask if it were possible that perhaps you had misremembered who you gave the cards to."

Gwyn looked affronted. "What is that supposed to mean?"

"I'm sorry. That may have come out wrong." Charlie backpedaled but could tell she'd struck a nerve of truth. Gwyn was protesting too much. "You first stated that you weren't sure who you'd given the papers too, but then you remembered Zeek."

She nodded as if to back up that as the truth.

"There is no one who works here by that name."

Gwyn's widened. "But—"

Charlie decide to take a risk, hoping that she wouldn't get herself in trouble. Instead of tugging on the string, she yanked. "Why did you make that up, Miss Milford?

"I didn't—"

"We both know you did." Charlie gentled her tone. "I just want to know what you really remembered from that night."

Gwyn's bottom lip trembled, but she covered it by taking another sip of her drink. "I might have misremembered some things."

Charlie tamped down the urge to smile in triumph. She'd known the woman's sudden memory of the man she'd spoken to had come too easily. "Why don't you tell me what really happened?"

"Okay, but you've got to understand why I said what I did." Gwyn took a fortifying breath. "Katherina is amazing, truly one of the greatest actresses of our time, and *I* get to work for her. It's a huge privilege, and I feel like I'm a breath away from losing that job almost every day."

Charlie watched as the woman composed herself with a few deep breaths as if she were on the verge of losing it.

"Clearly you're a good assistant or she wouldn't have brought you here with her," Charlie said.

"True. She's kept me on longer than most. I just can't make mistakes, you know? And the cards—that was a mistake."

"Tell me what happened."

Gwyn pressed her arms straight on the chair and tucked her chin as if preparing herself for the truth. "I got the first batch printed off just fine."

"First batch?" Charlie wasn't sure if it was procedure to have multiple copies just in case.

Gwyn flushed. "I printed them off and then went to get a coffee. I then proceeded to accidentally spill that coffee." She shrugged as if to say, *What can you do?*

"I see. So you needed to get another set printed."

"Yes, but by that time, I had to pick up Katherina's dress for the gala. I couldn't be in two places at once, so I asked Raji to reprint them and make sure they got to the podium."

"Raji White?" Charlie clarified.

Gwyn nodded. "He's Elliot's best friend from, like, childhood, I think? I got to know him some while on set and I just didn't want to throw him under the bus like that, you know? He'd never do anything like this."

"You mean the threat?"

"Threat?" Gwyn frowned. "What do you mean?"

Charlie hesitated. She had expected Katherina to tell her assistant what the cards said, but it seemed as if she'd kept the extent of the threat to herself.

"The cards."

Gwyn frowned but didn't push for more info. It seemed as if she was happy to stay in the dark. "Yeah. Raji and I cover for each other all the time. I mean, he's not Elliot's assistant, but he might as well be, you know?"

"How so?"

"He does whatever Elliot needs him to. Get him food, be his camera guy for social media, fill out his taxes," she laughed, obviously not meaning the last one. "But Elliot seems really cool with him."

"After you spilled coffee on the first cards, how was Raji supposed to get the second set?"

"The USB." She reached in the outer pocket of her purse but frowned. "I told him to print them off and then stick the drive back into my purse whenever he could. I've seen him several times, so he should have put it back."

"Did it have anything else on it?"

Gwyn visibly swallowed. "Yeah. Like a lot of things. Katherina's schedule, other speeches she's got to give, things like that. Nothing super personal—no bank stuff, you know? But still, important things." Gwyn dropped her head into her hands. "She's going to kill me."

Charlie felt bad for the young woman who was clearly nervous about losing her job.

"I'll look into it for you," she found herself saying. This was beyond what she'd told Sophia she'd do, but she hated to see Gwyn so broken. "We'll make sure that it's recovered."

"Thanks." Gwyn sniffed and wiped under her eyes where a few tears had fallen. "Who are you again?"

Charlie offered a warm smile. "Resort staff."

"This seems above and beyond your job," Gwyn laughed.

"I used to be a private investigator. I'll see what I can do." Charlie stood, noticing the widening of the young woman's eyes. "And let's keep this chat between us for now—unless the police ask for information, of course."

Gwyn nodded. "Okay."

"Thank you for being honest with me."

She nodded again, and Charlie left her with her fruity drink under the shade of the umbrella.

Gwyn had lied to save her position. Was it possible that lie had hidden the true culprit?

5

THE TIGHTNESS in Charlie's shoulders relaxed the minute her toes sunk into the white sand. The Sunday evening influx of beachgoers was less than she'd expected, and somehow Charlie felt both a part of and separate from the chaos of the Pearl Sands Resort as she made her way toward the southern end of the tied island.

When she'd first come to Barnabe Island, where the resort was located, she'd passed the opulent homes that occupied the northernmost area of the land-tied island. They were multi-million-dollar homes, and each one looked like something out of a home magazine. Then she'd seen the resort and thought *it* looked like something from a magazine or movie as well.

The resort itself occupied the island's central area, as well as the beachfront there, but it was the southernmost area that she liked to explore best. There, the residents lived in modest homes with small shops scattered about. They had their own portion of beach along with a small pier. It created a type of natural cove where old, and sometimes broken down, boats were harbored.

She knew the contrast with the resort and expensive homes to the north was drastic, but she'd found some of the most authentic and genuinely kind people in the small village on Barnabe Island. She often found herself retreating there when she needed a break from the opulence.

A few resort guests waved at her, and she recognized them from the excursions she'd booked for them. Others went about their beach-time with abandon. Some sunbathed in the waning light, others played frisbee or volleyball, while others still strolled along the water like Charlie was.

While she didn't always have the weekends free, she had taken half of Sunday off to recover from the gala. The planning had been spectacular and, while she still had more to do for the week leading up to the premiere, things were in motion. Charlie felt less like she was running in a rat race and more like she was walking a prepared path.

The sun dipped lower and painted the sky in brilliant yellows, oranges, and pinks. A true Floridian sunset complete with the shadow of overhead palm trees and the sound of music up ahead. Charlie's stomach growled as she caught the scent of carne asada and fresh lime. It was time for drinks and food.

"Charlie, there you are." Valerie came out on the patio of *La Cantina* with a drink in hand. She wore a bright yellow wrap dress with huge pink flowers all over it, and her hair was pulled up into a high ponytail. Everything Valerie did seemed elegant to Charlie, who wore long shorts and a flowy tank top.

"Sorry. Am I late?" Charlie took in the packed patio. Bistro lights hung overhead and illuminated the beautiful Mexican art on the walls.

"Right on time. Come on in." Valerie put her arm around Charlie's shoulders and leaned close. "Hope you don't mind, but we invited Nelson."

Charlie tried not to react. She failed.

"Oh, that was a bad idea, huh?"

"No. Not really."

Valerie pulled them to the side of the door leading inside. "What happened between you two? I was sure there was *something* brewing, but then it all changed."

Charlie hadn't talked to her friend about their slight falling out—if you could call it that—at the art gallery opening, but she'd thought about it plenty. Instead of rehashing it now, she just said, "We're just friends like we've always been."

Valerie narrowed her eyes but instead of pushing, she nodded once. "Then let's get some dinner."

Loud music played over hidden speakers as the women walked into the crowded space. Resort workers, groundskeepers for the wealthy that lived on the north side, and the residents of the southern half of the island filled every table and booth. It was a beautiful mix of ages and ethnicities, and Charlie loved it.

She far preferred *La Cantina's* atmosphere to that of the upscale restaurants at the resort, but it wasn't always feasible for her to make it down the beach. When she did though, she always got the same thing.

"Let me guess..." Telma gently bumped her shoulder against Charlie's as she walked past with a tray filled with chips and salsa. "Tacos again?"

Charlie laughed. "You know it."

"Have a seat. I'll be there soon." Telma winked and bustled off.

"You could branch out, you know," Valerie said. She pointed out the small table in the corner. "There are so many good things on this menu."

"I know. And one day, I will. But until then, I'm going to have my fill of the amazing tacos."

They approached the table, and Stephen looked up with a wide smile. Nelson soon followed suit. Despite everything, Charlie's stomach still tightened at the sight, and she sensed her cheeks flooding with warmth. He was handsome, she knew that, but why did her body have to react like a schoolgirl's?

"Evening." She slipped into the empty seat next to Nelson as Valerie reclaimed hers alongside her husband.

"Glad you could make it," Stephen said. He was always the most energetic of their bunch, and the most easygoing. "Is it tacos again?"

Charlie laughed. "Yes. Yes, it is. And I'm proud of it. They are some of the best tacos I've ever had."

"Glad to hear it," Telma said. She handed out waters and efficiently took their orders before winking at Charlie and turning back to the kitchen.

"What did I miss?" Charlie asked, spooning salsa onto a chip. It crunched delightfully in her mouth, and the flavors washed over her tongue with bright notes from the tomatoes and a depth of flavor that added spice but not so much heat it was unbearable. It was perfection.

"Not much. Just plans for Stephen's sabbatical coming up next year, travel destinations, and Nelson here telling us he's basically been everywhere." Valentina eyed him and reached for her own chip, choosing the queso instead.

"I really haven't." Nelson's eyebrow rose. "It just so happens that I've been to all of the locations on your list. That's all."

"What places are they?" Charlie asked.

Valentina rattled off a list of the most desirable vacation destinations, and Charlie laughed. "I've been to them all too."

"You have?" Nelson looked genuinely surprised.

"I love to travel." Charlie thought back to her most-recent trip the year previous when she traveled to rural Italy. She'd done the basic areas like Rome, Venice, and Florence, but she wanted a real-life experience and met a pen-pal on a website. She shared the story with her friends and added, "Bianca was lovely and so kind to let me stay with her. We ate gelato every night in the town square, and I took long walks through the countryside. It was a trip I'll never forget."

Her gaze shifted to rest on Nelson's rapt attention. "You really did that? Just up and went to Italy to stay with a woman you'd never met. She could have been a serial killer."

Everyone laughed, but Charlie protested. "Hardly. Besides, you forget. I'm a PI and know how to vet people. I connected with her on Facebook and was able to verify her identity through several of her friends using various...*means*."

She'd reached out to some of them pretending to be someone she was not in order to verify that Bianca really was who she said she was. Not one of them had any information that made her believe Bianca was anyone other than a sweet woman from Italy.

"Did you pay her?" Stephen asked, clearly more curious about how the whole thing worked than if she'd been in danger.

"No. She was just a gracious host. But I did pay for our meals out and invited her to stay with me any time. Though now that I'm at the resort, I may have to think of something else if she takes me up on that." Charlie laughed, trying to figure out where Bianca would stay if she came to her small cottage.

"If she does come, let me know. You two can borrow my house." Nelson's kind smile and even kinder gesture melted the last of Charlie's resolve. She offered him a true smile—perhaps the first she'd given since that night of the art gallery.

Their food arrived, and most of the conversation stilted as they dug into the large plates filled with rice, beans, and their various entrees.

"The tacos are amazing, as always," Charlie said, feeling the need to share to prove her point.

Everyone nodded, and their chatter resumed. Stephen shared a few funny anecdotes from his classes that day, Valentina talked about plans she had for the rest of the week and the high-profile guests they were serving, and Charlie shared some of her responsibilities for the rest of the week, but Nelson was strangely absent from the conversation. He chimed in here and there, but not with anything substantial.

By the time their plates had been cleared and Valentina was at the end of her second mojito, Stephen declared it was time for him to drive them home so Valentina could crash on the couch and watch her favorite reality television shows.

"But we could go dancing," Val said, her words slightly slurred.

"You don't dance, honey. Trust me."

She looked at him, blinking for a minute, before she broke into a smile. "I love you, Stephen."

"You too, honey." He turned aside to Nelson and Charlie with a dramatic whisper, "I'd better get her home."

They laughed and watched as Valentina leaned against Stephen as he ushered them out the side door.

"They're cute," Charlie said, the words slipping out before she could rethink how young they made her sound—and feel.

"They are," Nelson agreed, oblivious to her internal thoughts. His deep sigh following the words clued her in to something else.

"Nelson, what's going on?"

"What?" He turned to her, meeting her gaze as if he'd been a million miles away and had only just come back to their conversation.

"There's clearly something wrong." She wanted to say more, to convince him she was still his friend even if things were strained at the moment, but she bit her cheek. Best to see what he would say next before opening her mouth wide enough for her foot to fit.

"I'd hoped it wasn't too obvious."

"So something *is* wrong."

"Not wrong, exactly. Today is a…difficult day."

"In what way?" She refrained from reaching across the table and resting her hand on his. *Baby steps, Charlie.*

"It is—was—my anniversary." Nelson turned to look out the window, pain etched on his handsome features.

"I'm sorry." She wasn't sure what to say. She'd loved and lost once herself, but that had been years ago and he hadn't been a spouse, just a boyfriend. Not that loss played favorites over titles.

While the pain was never fully gone, it didn't mean she was an expert. Far from it. She'd closed herself off for so long, she'd started to wonder if she'd ever be able to open up again.

"It's… Maybe I'm just too introspective for my own good, but every year, it comes around and it's hard, no matter what I do. I thought dinner with friends would overshadow it, and it did—"

"But not enough."

He shrugged. "What's enough? What is an acceptable amount of missing the woman I'd loved?" He winced as if he'd said too much.

"Tell me about her," Charlie said.

"Her name was Gabriella, and she was beautiful and so funny. We met while running a half-marathon. She tripped and skinned up her knee, and I used part of my shirt to bandage it. We both came in last, but it was love at first sight." He gave a humorless laugh. "I know, that sounds so cliché, and it is, but it was our story."

"You're lucky to have found a love like that."

He met her gaze then, his eyes softening to a light brown. "I am. It's been ten years since she passed, but it still gets me. Most days, I'm fine, but not our anniversary."

There was a world of questions Charlie wanted to ask, but she held them back. The conversation she'd had with Sophia Perez came back to her, and she wanted to know more. Had Gabriella also been a cop? How long were they married? How did she die?

The questions died on her lips as Nelson tossed his napkin on the table.

"I'm sorry. I'm probably not the best company right now." He scooted his chair back.

"You can go, I understand, but just know I'm here if you'd like to talk." Charlie made sure he saw the willingness in her expression.

He paused as if he might take her up on that, but instead he pursed his lips, nodded once, and left.

THE SOUND of seagulls woke Charlie the next morning. Light filtered in through the window of her room between palm fronds that cast shadows on the wall in front of her. It was one of things she liked most about the room—the morning light.

Yawning and throwing her arms over her head in a spine-cracking stretch, Charlie stayed in bed for a few minutes longer, lost in thought.

She replayed Nelson's words from the night before, the small look into his former life shining a light on the man much like the images on her wall. There were hidden depths to him—something Charlie wasn't surprised to find—but she wondered what else still lay beneath the surface.

The memory of her conversation with Sophia replayed in her mind. How the detective had admitted she was Nelson's sister-in-law, the cause for her casual, if at times abrupt, treatment of him, but also that her sister had died.

Charlie didn't know much more than that. It was obvious Nelson had loved Gabriella, but what made his grief so fresh years after his wife's passing?

Charlie made a face. Her thoughts sounded cold even to herself. She was allowing her analytical brain to take over, and the compassion she should have for him was absent. Who said there was a number on grief? Why couldn't a man mourn the loss of his beloved years after she'd passed?

That wasn't it, though. Charlie rubbed her face. There had been an underlying current to his words that she'd picked up on. She'd wanted to press, but last night clearly wasn't the time to do that.

Then again, was there a time for it? She'd pushed Nelson away and, at first, she'd thought that was to protect herself. Was it possible there was a hidden motivation to her actions?

Her phone beeped a reminder, and she pushed herself from the comfort of her bed. She showered, dressed, and had breakfast in record time before checking her calendar again. Today, there was a brunch for the cast and a meet-and-greet folded into the second half. Fans of the stars who had won—or paid for—a slot would be introduced to them in a controlled environment before being allowed to screen the movie early. Each big-name star was to be in attendance at the brunch, though they weren't required to watch the movie until the actual preview. Hopefully, the meet-and-greet would be the perfect opportunity for her to connect with Raji White and ask about what happened to the cards and USB.

Charlie wanted to believe that he was innocent in all of this, caught up in it only for the simple fact that he'd had the responsibility of printing the second set of cards, but it was hard to tell the truth from the lie. It was completely possible he or Gwyn—or both—had lied about the cards. But why?

Charlie planned to get to the truth today.

Slipping on her black flats, she slung her purse over one shoulder and headed out the door to her desk in the lobby. The morning responsibilities were Juliana's to take care of, but Charlie wanted to make sure the young woman had all that she needed. They had VIP guests staying at the resort that week and Charlie didn't want the young woman getting overwhelmed by too many new tasks so early in her new position.

"How are things this morning?" Charlie asked, dropping her bag into one of the spare seats in front of the desk she shared with Juliana. They found that trading off shifts tended to work best for them, and this week was no different.

Juliana held up a finger before picking up the ringing phone. "Concierge desk, this is Juliana speaking. How may I help you?"

Charlie smiled, content to wait as the young woman performed her duties. Juliana covered the mouthpiece and whispered, "This is the third time this guest has called."

Charlie saw the barely contained frustration simmering and held out her hand for the headset. "Hello, this is the head of concierge." Charlie rolled her eyes to show Juliana she wasn't being serious but taking on a role. "May I ask who's speaking?"

The guest mentioned her name, but it wasn't familiar to Charlie. She handled the client, ensuring that they had all they needed this time around, and then hung up the phone.

"I'm sorry." Juliana's soft features were pinched with worry.

"Nothing to be sorry about." Charlie took a seat in the extra chair and leaned forward. "One thing I've come to realize in this job is that questions are king. What I mean by that is a guest will often *think* they've got everything they need, but there are things they'll think of after hanging up. It's our job to consider every aspect and either provide what they need without their request or ask them about it."

"How do you know what they want?" Juliana looked as if she were seconds away from grabbing a blank piece of paper to write down what Charlie was about to say.

"Let's use this guest as an example." Charlie considered Juliana. "What was her first call about?"

"She wanted a special excursion for her husband for their anniversary."

"And was it going to end around dinnertime?"

"I— Yes." Juliana looked surprised.

"Then her next phone call was…"

"About dinner reservations." Juliana nodded. "Of course. I should have anticipated that."

Charlie smiled back at her. "This is completely new to you so you're not going to think of everything, but consider the points people usually care about. What do they need to bring to be prepared? What should they wear? Will there be food? Things like that. I tried to do that with this last call, and I think we got the rest squared away."

"Thank you for doing that." Juliana let out a sigh. "I'm learning, it's just taking time."

"I was an investigator for most of my life, things like this come naturally to me. Don't be too hard on yourself. Now, what else can we do?"

Charlie spent the next few hours going over items that Julianna was still growing accustomed to—scheduling larger parties, how to get around sold-out dinner reservations for important guests, and other boring details they had to have squared away by the end of the week.

When it was time for the brunch to start, Juliana left to go on her break. Charlie made sure the woman knew to call if anything came up that she didn't feel equipped to handle and then headed off toward the secluded pool they often used for events.

One of the security guys was stationed at the entrance to the pool and asked to see Charlie's identification, despite the fact she was wearing the Pearl Sands resort polo. She was tempted to chew the young man out, wondering if Ben had put her on some non-friendly list, but he merely looked at her ID, then at a list on his phone, and allowed her through.

Her incensed response sent off a claxon in her mind. She needed to give Ben the benefit of the doubt. It made sense that even hotel staff would be checked before being allowed into any part of the premiere events. Just because they worked at the resort didn't automatically mean that they could be allowed anywhere.

Taking in a breath and smoothing down her shirt, Charlie put on a smile and joined the other staff members at the food tables.

"How are things looking?" The attendant she spoke to was a familiar young woman, but Charlie couldn't remember her name. Thankfully, that wouldn't be necessary for this interaction.

"Good, Ms. Davis. The appetizers are out as requested at this time, though I'm afraid most of the event attendees aren't here yet."

Charlie looked around. The appetizers were in a shaded area, but she knew the heat would only increase as the day went on. Fans above swirled around the warming air and trays of ice had been placed beneath the dishes that needed to remain extra cool.

"I think it'll be all right. I hear stars are notorious for being late," she added in a stage whisper.

The young woman smiled. "I hear that too."

Charlie checked her watch and saw that it was ten minutes past the start time. While the stars brunch was to be followed by the meet-and-greet, Charlie was worried no one was going to show up.

Just then, commotion at the gate drew her attention. It was Elliot and Raji followed closely by a security guard and

Gwyn. Elliot paused to talk to Raji and then turned to enter the private pool area with Gwyn in tow. Raji disappeared from view, and Charlie felt the immediate tug to follow him.

Doing one last visual check that everything was in order, she unobtrusively stepped out past the security guy and went in search of Raji.

She didn't have to go far when she spotted him at one of the bars that also had a swim-up area. He'd just picked up a tall, fruity looking drink from the bar when she approached him.

"Mr. White?"

He squinted, taking a moment to place her, but she saw when he caught sight of the resort logo on her polo. "Uh, yeah?"

"May I have a few minutes of your time? I've got a few questions about some cards you printed for Ms. Kent."

His eyes bulged. "Y-yeah. Sure."

She followed him through a maze of unoccupied lounge chairs toward the shade on the side opposite the bar and private pool area. On the way, a familiar voice called out to her.

"Charlie, dear!"

Her stomach clenched. It was Ramona and, as much as she wanted to stop and talk, she knew this time was crucial to speak with Raji to hear his side of what happened with the cards and the USB.

"Hey, Ramona," she said. Raji slowed in front of her and relief swept through her. He would wait for her quick hello and good-bye to Ramona.

"Raji, did you bring that for me?"

"No, Mrs. Munter." Raji laughed. "This one's all mine. But I can get you one if you want?"

"Oh no, dear. It looks like you two have things to discuss. I just like to give you a hard time. And remember, next time, I'm not going to go easy on you."

"I wouldn't expect you to," he said. His demeanor said he was deferring to her in a humble, almost respectful, way.

"See you later, Charlie," Ramona said. She pulled her sunglasses down again and laid back against her lounge chair.

They continued on and Charlie asked, "How do you know Ramona?"

"She knows Ms. Kent somehow," he explained. "I found myself almost losing my shirt to her in poker last night." He laughed.

"Rumor is she's ruthless."

"It's not a rumor." He laughed again. "If we didn't have that brunch, I might have gotten the upper hand, but Elliot needed to get a few hours of sleep. She's already told me we're on for a rematch, though. I don't know if my wallet can keep up."

They stopped in front of a pair of unoccupied chairs and sat down.

"You didn't need to be at the brunch today?" she asked, making conversation as he got himself settled across from her with his drink on a small table between them.

"Nah. Elliot only needs me when we're on set, usually."

"That's an exciting job. How did you get into this line of work?"

Raji smiled, and she noticed a set of identical dimples. "It's not really work. We're like, you know, homeboys."

She wasn't sure what that meant. "Friends?"

"Yeah. Since kindergarten."

"That's incredible. And what is it exactly that you do for him?"

Her tone must have alerted him to the serious turn of her questions because he frowned and looked up at her, tearing his gaze away from his drink. "Who are you again?"

"My name is Charlie Davis and I work at the Pearl Sands. I'm looking into the issue that arose with Ms. Kent's speech cards."

"And you talked to Gwyn." His shoulders slumped.

"While she was hesitant to give anything away, I assured her I'm only trying to get to the bottom of this and who might want to threaten Ms. Kent."

"That's what it was? On the cards?" He leaned forward, more a curious onlooker than involved party. Or was it an act?

"Why don't you start by telling me what happened with the cards."

He shrugged and laid back against the lounge cushion. "It was all pretty standard. I mean, Gwyn and I have been helping each other out since being on set and when she said that she needed a favor, I did it."

"You printed off the new cards and then you gave her back the flash drive?"

He frowned. "I put it in the pocket of her purse."

"What did you do with the cards?" Charlie still felt like something was missing.

"I slid them into the slot on the podium. I'm pretty sure there were a few security guys there when I did it too."

Charlie had checked and they had seen him.

"Then what?"

"That was it." He shrugged and took along sip of his drink. "I mean, I don't know what happened after that, but I was with Elliot for the rest of the night until he got to his room and I went to mine. They're adjacent."

"I see." Charlie frowned. "Do you have any idea who would want to threaten Ms. Kent?"

"No way. She's cool. I mean, a little uptight on set, but what actor isn't? There's a lot going on."

He appeared genuine, and Charlie had no reason to doubt what he was saying. Then again, she didn't know much about the movie industry.

"Here's my card." She slipped him her resort business card. "Please call me if you think of anything that might be helpful."

"Uh, sure. I mean, what's going to happen? Or is it just business as usual?"

It was a valid question—even a good one—but Charlie wasn't sure how to answer it. She chose the truth. "I don't know, Mr. White."

6

CHARLIE LEFT Raji White drinking his fruity drink in the shade of an umbrella. She had more questions than she'd gotten answers, but that seemed to be how most cases went. Diving deep into the unknown until it became understood.

She was about to go back toward the brunch crowd, even though she'd just be an extra body there and not exactly useful, when she caught sight of a figure she recognized. Thornton Blackwell walked across the pool area looking like he was heading to the Kentucky Derby.

He was well-dressed in a light tan linen suit with a baby-blue collared shirt and a smart hat paired with dark glasses. The blood red cravat at his neck made Charlie uneasy for some reason, but she shook it off and trotted after the man.

"Mr. Blackwell?" Charlie called out. She picked up her pace through the slowly growing number of pool guests. "Excuse me, Mr. Blackwell?"

He paused halfway down the outdoor corridor that led toward the beach and turned to watch as she approached. A faint smile hinted at recognition, but he remained aloof. "Yes?"

"I'm Charlie Davis." She flashed a smile. "I'm looking into the mysterious notecards that were given to Ms. Kent at the gala."

His eyes flashed with recognition. "Ah, yes. Are you with resort security?"

"Not exactly." She was never sure how to handle this question. "I'm a licensed private investigator in the state of Florida, and the resort manager has asked me to look into this—discreetly." She hoped the addition of her discretion would put the man's fears at ease, and it seemed to.

"I see. That sounds wise. How can I help you?" He shifted to face her more fully, and she finally placed the somewhat British accent he had. It reminded her of a man she'd known who had grown up in London to expat parents who'd brought him back to America in his teens. Not quite British, but not American either. It made Charlie wonder at his story, but that wasn't why they were talking.

"I wanted to ask you a few questions. I will need to speak with Ms. Kent herself, but I'm sure you know her well, and I had hoped to narrow down my questions so that when we do speak, it will be less of an inconvenience for her." This wasn't the heart of why she wanted to speak with him, but she hoped it was close enough to the truth not to make the man suspicious.

In reality, anyone who had access to Katherina's cards could be considered a suspect for the swap.

"That is an excellent point. Please, ask away."

She appreciated his seeming openness. "I ask everyone this, but do you know of anyone who would want to see harm come to Ms. Kent? Or, if not harm exactly, someone who might want to scare her?"

"Heavens no. Katherina—that is, Ms. Kent—is very kind to everyone she works with. On set and off, I don't know of anyone that would want to see harm come to her, or anything else." He straightened his shoulders.

"What about someone that may want to steal her necklace?"

He frowned. "That's rather on the nose, don't you think?"

"Perhaps," she admitted. "But I need to ask."

"Yes, of course you would. I can't think of anyone that might…" He trailed off.

Charlie's senses heightened and she leaned forward. "What is it? What did you just think of?"

"It's not so much that she would want the neckless exactly, but..." He was talking to himself at this point. "But perhaps she would."

"Who, Mr. Blackwell?" Charlie pressed.

"Miss Milford." He looked around as if the mention of her name could summon her. "I don't like to speak ill of anyone, and she has been a very hard worker, but I can't help but think Gwyn isn't with Ms. Kent due to any loyalty."

"What do you mean?" Charlie asked.

"I'm not always around, naturally, but on set, I've noticed several times that Gwyn will be gone for stretches of time and I'll often find her chatting with one director or another—or perhaps someone close to them. I'd wager she's looking for a bigger career than what she's let on, but it's a delicate thing, this business. She could get a big role if the right people pick her, but she could also fade into oblivion if Katherina says one word to the wrong person."

"What would that have to do with Ms. Kent's necklace, though?"

He flashed what Charlie could only describe as a bittersweet smile. "Ms. Kent looked, dare I say, foolish up there on stage. She was clearly taken aback, and it won't truly tarnish her reputation, but enough foibles and directors will start to wonder. I don't want to think it of Gwyn, but perhaps this was planned?"

Charlie knew the man had made a good point—and a valid one—but had Gwyn lied to her when she said that Raji had printed off the second copies? That would mean Raji was lying for her. Perhaps she'd gone up to write on the cards while they were unattended in the podium. But that didn't track. She assumed the security guy, who had confirmed seeing Raji, would have mentioned seeing a beautiful young woman at the podium.

"That does make a sad sort of sense," Charlie finally said out loud.

"Again, I couldn't say this with certainty and wouldn't want to tarnish Gwyn's reputation. She is quite adept at acting, and she's been a great help to Katherina, but I don't know that she has what it takes to make it in this industry."

"And what is that, Mr. Blackwell?"

He smiled. "If I knew that, I'd be a much richer man, Ms. Davis."

She watched as he tipped his hat and walked away. He hadn't asked if she had more questions, he'd just determined that their time was up.

Then again, she wasn't sure what else she could ask him. He'd been seated at the table where Ms. Kent's things were set and would have no reason to harm his client's reputation—unless he had one she didn't know about.

Charlie considered his quick leap to throwing Gwyn at Charlie as if she were a shiny new lead for her to follow, eclipsing all other options. Had that been a ploy? Or had it been genuine?

Charlie sighed and turned back to the private pool area. She'd take what Mr. Blackwell said along with the other information she'd gathered. That was the only way to truly know if something was viable or just coming from a vivid imitation.

For now, Charlie would rub shoulders with movie stars and consider why someone would want to frighten Katherina Kent in front of a room full of people.

CHARLIE LEFT the brunch early after most of the bigger stars had left. The leftover group was filled with giggling fans who had indulged a little too much at the open mimosa bar.

After checking in with Juliana that she wasn't needed in the lobby, her next stop was her least-favorite place in the resort: the security office.

Facing the nondescript tan door off the main pool area with hunched shoulders, Charlie knocked and waited to be granted entrance. It took the young security guard almost a full minute before he stuck his head out and eyed her skeptically.

"Yeah?"

Charlie knew better than to berate the young man for his less-than-professional manner, but she still had to bite the inside of her cheek before she responded. "I'd like to speak with Ben, please."

"Director Simmons isn't available for meetings at the moment."

Charlie had worked with difficult people before. She also knew she was prone to having a bit of a temper. Perhaps it was the young man's use of *director* or just the fact that Ben had likely told him not to let Charlie in, but her anger was kindled, and she didn't know if she could stop the frustration from surfacing.

"Could you please go and ask *Ben* if he could spare five minutes to meet with me regarding Ms. Kent and the directive Mr. Delgado has given me. Thank you." She forced an over-bright smile that might have looked more menacing than appreciative, but the young man didn't blink. He just shrugged and left, closing the door on her.

Almost three minutes later, he came back and beckoned her to follow him.

This wasn't her first time in the security offices, and she walked past the familiar bank of monitors that flicked between locations all over the resort to a corridor that led to Ben's office.

She always felt a little like she was entering a cave when she came to see him, but she wouldn't let the fact that she was on his turf cow her. What she'd told the young man was true. She had been tasked with uncovering who was trying to frighten Ms. Kent and if the threat was real. That was the only reason she was here.

"Ms. Davis, what can I do for you?"

Ben sat behind a large oak desk with two monitors, like a king surveying his land. She knew he didn't like her—or perhaps it wasn't so much about like or dislike, but he certainty distrusted her. She had a feeling he thought she needed to keep to her own work and butt out of his. If Felipe hadn't been involved, she might have agreed, but when their boss—the one overseeing the whole resort—suggested something, that had to stand. Petty differences couldn't get in the way.

Charlie squared her shoulders. "I'm not sure where cameras are placed on the resort, but I was wondering if you've got a video feed from the ballroom from the time before the gala. I already spoke with a few of the guards on duty, but if there's a recording, it's possible it caught something your men did not."

"I suppose you'd like one of my men to look through it? Try to find some type of lead for you?"

Charlie blinked. "I— No. That's not what I was asking at all. First, I'd like to know if there even *was* video surveillance in there, and then if there was, I was going to look through it."

"I see." Ben leaned forward, steepling his fingers together. "I actually don't know."

She ground her teeth. Tamping down her frustration, she kept her voice calm and even. "Is there a way to find out?"

Ben held her gaze and then reached for his phone. "Skylar. Yeah, is there a feed for South Sea Ballroom and, if so, was it activated during the day of the gala?"

She waited as he waited, his finger tapping lightly against the dark green blotter that covered his desk. Charlie noticed he hadn't even offered her a seat, but that was just like Ben. He seemed to take pleasure in inconveniencing her in any way possible, or perhaps he was hoping she would break and he'd be able to tell her off to Felipe.

That's not happening.

"Okay. Is that right?" Ben spoke, still avoiding her gaze. "I see. Well...okay."

He hung up, and she watched as an almost imperceptible frown drew his eyebrows down before he forced them back up.

"Bad news?" Charlie watched him carefully.

"We do have cameras there—they are almost everywhere in the resort—but those ones weren't monitored. Of course, when the event began, they began recording. It's typical of a big resort like this to not record all images, especially in an area that isn't heavily trafficked most of the time."

It sounded like Ben was trying to justify it, but she brushed it off and decided to give him the professional courtesy. "That's unfortunate, but it makes sense. There's no one else I could talk to, is there?" She kept her voice light in hopes that he wouldn't feel attacked.

"No. I think the rest of my guys were overseeing the new arrivals of our famous guests."

"I'm sure you've got your hands full. I'll check with my staff as well. Thanks." She turned to go, but Ben called out to her.

"Don't you think it would be in everyone's best interests for you to just…pick a side?"

"Side?" She turned to face him but kept her expression neutral.

"Security. Concierge. One or the other. It gives me whiplash, and I have to assume it confuses you." He gave what he probably thought was a sympathetic look, but which Charlie saw right through. He was goading her.

"I'm not sure you want me to pick, Ben." With a flat smile, she turned and left the security office, letting Ben stew over what she'd meant by that.

7

THE SOUND of crashing waves reached Charlie as she lay in bed. The lights were off and she'd cracked the window just a little to better hear the ocean. She couldn't sleep, and that wasn't like her. Usually by the time she'd read a chapter or two of the true crime story she was reading, she was able to turn off the lights, close her eyes, and be asleep within minutes.

Not tonight. Tonight, Charlie started on her back, rolled to one side then the other, and ended up on her back again without feeling even a little sleepy. There was a lot on her to-do list for the next day, and a good night's sleep was crucial to that, but sleep wouldn't come.

Her gaze shifted to the window and then to the ceiling faintly illuminated by the green numbers of her bedside alarm clock. It had been a long day, somewhat hectic at parts, but it hadn't been that much different than other days.

After her conversations with Raji and Thornton and the follow-up with Ben, Juliana had finally called her in to help with a difficult guest. She was more than happy to help, and then she'd taken over for the rest of the day as it was time for her shift to start. Juliana hadn't left behind much work, and Charlie now considered if that was part of why she was awake.

Was Juliana better suited for her job than she was?

Charlie knew she was good at what she did for the Pearl Sands. Her experience as a detective gave her a leg up that set them apart in the hotel industry, but was it enough? Would it be better to let Juliana take over? She was the one with a degree in the field, unlike Charlie.

She turned on her side again and pushed her pillow more firmly under her head. The truth settled uncomfortably in the pit of her stomach. She was thinking about what Ben had said.

Did she need to pick a side? Either work security or concierge, not both?

The memory of Felipe begging her on several occasions to help him get to the bottom of crimes at the hotel halted the thoughts, though it didn't stop them. She should consider all aspects of this and—

Her cellphone rang, jolting her from her thoughts. She scrambled across the bed to the nightstand and pulled it free from the charging cord. The clock read 2:33, and the caller ID showed a familiar name.

"Ramona?"

"I'm sorry to w-wake you, Charlie." Ramona's voice shook.

Charlie ignored the fact that she hadn't been asleep. "What's wrong?"

"My jewelry. It's been stolen."

Charlie jumped to her feet. "Are you safe? Is there someone in your room?"

"No. Yes. I mean, yes, I'm safe. No, no one is in my room...now."

Charlie got up and stepped into a pair of jean shorts. "I'll be right over. Did you call security?"

"No, and I don't want to." Ramona sounded more certain now.

"Why not? This is a hotel security issue."

"I know, but..." She took a breath. "Can we talk first?"

Charlie could hardly make her call them when it was her property and her room that was in question. "I'll be over in five minutes. Don't open the door for anyone but me."

"Of course not." Some of Ramona's indignation came out, and Charlie felt better.

"I'll be right there." They hung up, and Charlie pulled on a clean t-shirt. She had no makeup on, but that was hardly an issue right then.

Slipping into a pair of flats she always left by the door, she grabbed a small flashlight she kept on a shelf nearby and headed out into the darkness. Her keys jingled as she slipped them into her pocket after locking the door behind her.

The walk to Ramona's villa took four minutes, but Charlie took the last minute to look around the back side of the villa that butted up to the beach. She'd been in this position before, though it had been a different villa that time, and she knew there were cameras that would have caught any movement—including her own at that moment.

Would security be alerted to her presence even now? Perhaps that would be better. If Ramona didn't want to call them, but they came of their own volition, Charlie couldn't be blamed.

"Ramona," she said, knocking on the door.

"There you are," she said, pulling the door open and ushering Charlie in.

It had only been six minutes, but it was clear the woman had counted each second as it passed. She clutched at the neck of her fuchsia silk bathrobe and looked up and down the empty walkway outside of the villa before closing and locking the door behind Charlie.

"What happened?" Charlie asked.

Ramona paced to the mini bar. "I need a drink first. You want something?"

"No, thank you."

Ramona shot her a look before pouring herself a generous glass of an amber-colored liquid. After a long drink, she appeared fortified and motioned for Charlie to join her at the sitting area.

"I almost always take a sleeping aid before I go to bed." Ramona took another long drink. "I didn't do that tonight because I was out late and by the time I got back, as well as factoring in when I had to wake up, it was too late. I didn't want to be groggy when I woke up."

Charlie nodded. "You're a light sleeper normally, then?"

"I don't even know, Charlie. If Siggy were here, he could tell you, but I almost always sleep with some sort of aid. Tonight, I didn't, and of course it was the night something happened."

"What *did* happen? And are you sure we shouldn't call up security for this?'"

"Not yet." Ramona skewered her with a look. "I took a bubble bath when I got back and had a few drinks and then I toppled in to bed. It was late, but for the first time in a long time, I wanted to sleep naturally. And I did. I fell asleep, and it was wonderful until I woke up to the sound of my door closing."

"You're sure it was in this villa?"

Ramona gave her a look. "I know what you're saying, but it was so loud. There was no way it *wasn't* in here. I mean, you know the other villas aren't close at all except for in the back patio area. I know it was my front door and it's a moot point anyway."

"Because your jewelry is missing."

"Right." Ramona's face paled, and she looked away. "I should have listened to Sigmond. He always tells me to use the hotel safe or, if not that, then at least put my valuables in the room safe."

"But you don't?" Charlie prompted after Ramona had fallen silent for a full minute.

"No. I...I just feel safe here."

"Show me." Charlie stood, and Ramona reluctantly did as well, teetering a little with the effects of the alcohol.

Charlie steadied her with an arm around her waist and they made their way to the bedroom. Ramona tossed out her hand, almost throwing herself off balance in the process, and pointed to the dresser. It sat directly across from the king-sized bed, and the top drawer was pulled out. Inside, Charlie could see rows and rows of velvet spacers meant to hold precious gems. They were empty.

"Oh, Ramona," she breathed.

Only one small earring back was left, and Charlie's stomach clenched. "Was it like this when you woke up?"

"No." Ramona shook her head. "Everything was closed, but I had this sense... I checked and found them empty."

"I'm so sorry." Charlie sent her friend a commiserating look. "I'm guessing you have an inventory of what was taken?"

"I do, but that's not the worst part."

Charlie spun to face her. "What is?"

"Two things, really. One is the fact I always keep my wedding ring in there." Ramona's eyes welled with unshed tears. "They took that."

"I'm so sorry." Charlie squeezed the woman's hand, bare without the somewhat ostentatious diamond ring she always wore. "What's the other worst part?"

"I was *in here* while they were stealing all of my gems. Sleeping like a fool. How could I have not woken up? Maybe I don't need those sleep aids in the first place."

"Don't be so hard on yourself," Charlie said. She gently tugged Ramona back to the living room so they could sit. "A thief's job is to be quiet, so I'm not surprised in the least that you didn't wake up. I am surprised they attempted it though, what with you being in the room."

Charlie thought through all of the things that didn't add up. The fact a thief knew the location of Ramona's gems. That they had access to her room. And the more obvious fact: they knew she took sleep aids. It was the only explanation for how a thief would be so bold.

There was no way the thief would have known she hadn't taken them that night, but if they were going to brazenly come in and steal her jewelry from under her nose, they had to feel confident she wouldn't wake up.

"Ramona, tell me this. Have you had anything strange happen in the last few nights?"

"Strange in what way? Certainly nothing like this."

"No." Charlie wrinkled her forehead. "More like odd occurrences. Things being misplaced. A door opened when you thought it was locked. Something like that."

"Not that I can..." She trailed off and tilted her head. "Actually, now that you mention it, I did lose my room card. Oh my goodness, how did I not think about that?"

"Did you report it to the front desk?"

Ramona blushed. "No. I have a second, naturally, and just thought I'd left it in a pair of pants I'd sent to the cleaners. I figured they'd return it with the pants." She rubbed a hand over her face.

Charlie nodded. "That's probably it."

"What do you mean?" It appeared the shock was somewhat wearing off, or the alcohol had taken the edge off.

"I would guess that the thief was able to get their hands on your card and somehow knew you took something to help you sleep. They've been watching you—or so I would guess."

Ramona's eyes went wide. "Is that supposed to make me feel better?"

"No, of course not. I'm sorry." Charlie shook her head. How could she be so careless to frighten the woman with that observation?

"Do you really think that's what happened?" Ramona leaned forward, her expression earnest.

"I think so. The person felt confident you wouldn't wake up tonight. They couldn't know you wouldn't take your pills. They expected to be long gone before now."

"But how?" Ramona turned toward the back of the villa that faced the beach. "There's cameras and security."

"I know. It seems very bold." Charlie's head tilted to the side.

"What? What did you just think of?"

"I think we need to call the police."

"No." Ramona was adamant, but Charlie knew something Ramona didn't. The detective she was going to call could be trusted to keep things discreet. And that was what they would have to do here, because nothing was as it seemed.

"You should have called immediately, Mrs. Munter." Detective Perez looked more casual than Charlie had ever seen her while on the job. It likely had something to do with the fact that their call had come in around three in the morning.

"I know. Charlie has chastised me enough about all of this, but you have to understand from my perspective how much I do *not* want a big to-do about this."

"It may be too late for that," Sophia said.

"Out." Ramona stood and pointed to the door. "Out now if that's how you're going to treat this. I don't *have* to have the police look into this."

"Just hold on, Mrs.— *Ramona*." Sophia used her first name and held out both hands in a placating manner. "Before you go refusing my help, let me get the lay of the land here." She relayed what Charlie had told her over the phone and then asked, "Did I miss anything?"

"That's about it, I think," Ramona said.

"Then it would seem Charlie is right. Someone has been watching—perhaps even planning—this for long enough to know your habits and for them to get a hold of one of your room cards." Sophia's brow furrowed and she turned to look at Charlie. "You think this is connected to the string of crimes in town?"

It was a question posed as a statement. "It's why I called. I think there's more going on here, and I want to know why."

"Why what?" Ramona asked.

"Why someone would outwardly threated Katherina Kent about her jewelry and then go to the trouble of stealing yours instead. Was hers a ploy or are you the ploy?"

Ramona frowned.

"That came out wrong." Charlie flashed an apologetic smile.

"Then what's the right way to look at this?" Sophia asked.

"Either Katherina's jewelry was never truly at risk and these crimes aren't connected, or they are but the attention was to be diverted to her."

"That sounds complicated," Ramona said. She leaned back, finishing her second drink. Charlie wanted to caution her on keeping a clear head but knew her suggestion would fall on deaf ears.

"Tell me more about how you think her threat wasn't real," Sophia said.

"I'm not to a conclusion yet, but I have been asking around regarding Ms. Kent. I almost want to say that the threat against her jewelry might be more of a mark against her career than it is the safety of her diamonds."

"That someone is trying to upstage her?" Sophia tapped her pen against her notepad.

"Perhaps. There could be other reasons I haven't uncovered yet, though."

"What about my jewelry?" Ramona sounded like a pouty child, but she had the good grace to look apologetic about it.

"Do you want me to file a report?" Sophia asked.

"We've been over that."

"I'll take that as a no," Sophia said.

"How about as a *not yet*," Ramona amended. "Let's give Charlie here some time to work her magic."

Charlie's eyes went wide. "I'm not sure I can solve a burglary case, but I can look into it."

"Is there anything I can do to help?" Sophia asked.

"Check the burglary records. See if any of them mention being stalked before it happened—or things that don't seem possible for a random burglar to know. That could help us narrow in on a specific MO of this thief."

"What about me? What can I do?" Ramona looked between them.

"Do you have any other valuables?" Sophia asked.

Ramona looked like she was going to say no but then nodded. "A few I hid." She looked almost ashamed.

"Why don't we get those to the room safe?" Charlie asked. She offered a hopeful smile. "It's good you still have something important, but we don't want to risk this person coming back."

"You don't think he would, do you?" Ramona looked afraid for the first time since Charlie had known her.

"No." Sophia spoke up this time. "For all the thief knows, they took everything you had. We've closed the blinds and double-checked all the doors. With that sliding glass door stop I brought, there won't be a way for anyone to get in."

The detective's words seemed to comfort Ramona. "Okay. Good. That's a good idea."

"Do you want me to stay?" Charlie asked.

Ramona met her gaze with a bleary one of her own. "I— No, I don't think so. I'm just going to go to bed and hopefully get to sleep again. Put this mess behind me for now."

"Just remember to send over that detailed list of everything that's missing." Sophia handed her a business card. "This email is best."

"I will."

"And, Ramona?" Sophia held the older woman's gaze. "If you think of anything or feel threatened again, you need to call hotel security. There's no guarantee that Charlie will be available, and I'm not close enough to do something. Do you understand?"

"I do." Ramona nodded solemnly. "I'm sorry to drag you both into this mess."

"Don't be," Charlie said. "We're happy to help you."

She eyed the detective, who nodded in agreement. "There may come a point where I can no longer keep this from my team, but I'll let you know if we get there."

"I understand. Good night, ladies."

Charlie and Sophia walked to the door and waited outside to hear Ramona set the locks in place. The door handle made an electronic *click,* and Charlie knew it was set.

"I'm sorry for calling you," Charlie said.

"No, you're not." Sophia kept her gaze ahead as they walked down the darkened path.

Charlie caught a hint of a smile on the detective's face. "Okay, maybe I'm not, but it was either call you or risk Ramona not saying anything to anyone."

"You really think this is connected to my cases?" Sophia sent her a sideways look.

"I can't be certain, but it makes more sense if they are connected. The resort is like a shining beacon for any and all thieves at this point. With the amount of press and the line of stars coming in and out, it's like grand central station for wealth."

"Is it really that different than the resort's everyday clientele, though?"

Charlie considered her words before answering. "I can't speak from years of experience, obviously, but I can say that the last few months, we've done a good job of keeping our high-profile guests *out* of the public's eye. That's what has me so nervous about all of this. If the thief did decide to ply his trade here, it would be like a literal goldmine of options."

"Yet they chose Ramona? Why her?"

"Or are there others who don't know yet that they were robbed?" Charlie countered.

Sophia bobbed her head from side to side as they turned toward Charlie's cottage. Charlie put the key in the lock and stepped inside, giving space for Sophia to join her. The detective slipped out of her tennis shoes and sunk onto the couch.

"I feel like there should be an increased security presence here—provided by our department—but Felipe wouldn't hear of it. He assured me that Mr. Simmons was competent to handle all of this, but Ramona won't call him? What's that about?"

Charlie didn't know the specifics as to why Ramona didn't like Ben, but she wondered if it had anything to do with her own interactions with the man in the past. Was Ramona reacting to that? Or something more personal?

"I can't tell you that, but I can say that I know Ben tries his best."

Sophia's eyes narrowed. "Which sounds like code for you think our presence here is needed."

"I didn't say that." Charlie handed Sophia a glass of water and took a seat in the chair opposite her. "I do think he's doing the best job he can with the resources he has."

"To be fair, those resources are numerous."

"True." Charlie nodded as she considered the top-of-the-line security cameras and systems in place at the resort. "But there's the other side of this to consider. That someone is banking on the fact that there is a cat burglar on the loose in town and they might fly under the radar—or get lumped in with them."

"What does it matter? If there is or isn't, we're still trying to find them," Sophia said.

"Either Ramona's theft is part of that or it's a distraction."

"To create chaos while they go after what they really want, you mean?"

Charlie shrugged. "It's possible."

"But elaborate." Sophia drained the rest of her water. "I suppose it would need to be if someone was breaking in to the resort. Even the villas have top-notch security."

"Which is why I'm surprised someone from the security office didn't come to check on Ramona." Charlie didn't like the sound of that.

"It would appear our thief found a way around the cameras. Are you sure you can't convince Ramona to let me look into this on more official channels?"

"I'll try." Charlie stifled a yawn.

Sophia leaned forward, elbows on her knees. "Tell me one more thing before I leave and go home to crash before my next shift. Have you talked to my brother-in-law recently?"

Charlie's head spun at the question. "Nelson?"

"Yes." Sophia studied Charlie's response. "You and him are still friends, right?"

Charlie nodded. "He seemed a little out of sorts the last time I saw him."

"That would make sense." Sophia ran a hand over her hair. "I feel bad for him."

"Why?" Even as she asked, Charlie knew it would sound odd. If they were friends, wouldn't Sophia expect her to know what was going on?

"I'm not surprised he hasn't told you." The detective sighed wearily. "We're coming up on the tenth anniversary of Gabriella's murder."

A breath *whooshed* from Charlie. She should have assumed it was related to his late wife's death, but they'd never truly spoken about *how* she died, only that she was gone. But murder?

"He doesn't handle the anniversary well—and I don't blame him—but it's going to be especially difficult with it hitting a decade."

"That's awful." The words to ask how it had happened sat on the tip of Charlie's tongue, but she held them back. It wasn't Sophia's story to share and, for some reason Charlie couldn't quantify, she wanted Nelson to be the one to tell her—should he ever feel that free.

"I just wanted to see if you had a chance to speak with him. I... It's hard for me too around this time. He lost a wife, but I lost my sister."

"I'm so sorry, Sophia. That has to be incredibly difficult."

"It is," she agreed. "But I've been able to put the bitter memories to the past and only kept hold of the sweet ones. Most of them, that is. I'm afraid Nelson hasn't been able to do that as well."

"It's understandable." Charlie thought of the man. He'd had his shop broken into, needed to replace most of his pottery, and then she and him had found themselves at odds as well. It was one blow after another and, while Charlie knew he'd played a role—albeit small—in their disagreement, she couldn't bring herself to hold that against him.

"I should get going." Sophia stood. "Thank you for calling me even though you didn't have to."

"I thought it was important that you were kept apprised of the situation."

"And I appreciate that. Night, Charlie."

She watched the detective disappear into the darkness of the early morning. Every muscle was weary and Charlie could feel her lack of sleep, but she couldn't help but think that it would still be difficult to rest knowing that the threat to the resort hadn't stopped with the cards. She only wondered what might happen next.

8

CHARLIE STOOD in line at the Sea View Café waiting to order her third cup of coffee for the day. She was dragging, but after the night she'd had, it was no surprise. After placing an order for an iced vanilla latte with an extra shot, she stood at the back of the open café where the floor-to-ceiling doors slid back into the wall to create a walk-out patio area.

The ocean winked back at her, light on waves making diamond shapes, with a stretch of white stand in between. That, and all of the resort guests stretched out on towels, under umbrellas, or splashing in the water.

It was picturesque, and she took a moment to center her chaotic, sleepy thoughts. The bleary, early morning disruption of Ramona's call had thrown her off on a week that was already incredibly busy, but Charlie was still glad her friend had called. While she felt guilty that she hadn't immediately taken Ramona's case to Ben, as she probably should have, she felt certain Felipe would understand and put the guest's wishes above protocol. Especially when Charlie knew Ramona wouldn't turn around and blame the Pearl Sands for her own choices.

Still, it would help to know what—if anything—had been on the security cameras around the time of the break-in. Was it possible the burglar hadn't been caught on camera?

And why Ramona's room? That was the burning question Charlie was dealing with as it circled around in her thoughts. Katherina Kent's incredibly expensive necklace had been threatened, yet Ramona was the one dealing with a theft?

Charlie picked up her phone, but her thumb hovered over the contact icon. Should she call Felipe and ask him if other robberies had been reported? It could tip off the fact that she knew of one already, but it was safter than going directly to Ben. She had a feeling he wouldn't let a casual question go without thoroughly investigating whatever it was Charlie wasn't telling him.

"I believe this is yours?"

The deep masculine voice drew her eyes up until they connected with familiar hazel ones. "Nelson."

Charlie accepted the coffee and watched as he took a sip from his own. "You were lost in thought."

"I was." Charlie bit back the urge to open up to him about everything. He had a keen mind and was insightful when it came to the actions of others. He could help her, but he was dealing with his own grief—

even though she was certain she wasn't supposed to know that.

"You look like you want to talk." His observation sharpened his gaze at her. "Do you have time?"

She watched as he motioned to a table in the shade of an aqua-colored umbrella on the patio. It was tempting, but she didn't want to betray Ramona's trust—or Sophia's, for that matter. Could she skirt around both issues and still appear to be sharing with him? It wasn't that she wanted to fool Nelson, but she also didn't want to bother him. Any insight he might have into her case could be invaluable, though.

"Yes."

His eyes narrowed further. "Are you sure?"

She smiled this time. "Positive."

Charlie followed Nelson as he wove through the small bistro tables and pulled out a chair for her. It was warmer on the patio, and she clutched her iced latte as if to draw some of the coolness from it. Fans from overhead blew warm air around, which helped with the heat, but Charlie almost regretted agreeing to sit and talk.

"You look tired." Nelson said it without preamble, but there was kindness in his eyes.

"I *am* tired." She bit her lip. "Couldn't sleep well."

"I'm sure a call at two in the morning didn't help."

Charlie's eyes widened. "What— How did you know?"

"Ramona told me. She and I take a morning yoga class on the beach sometimes. She said she thought you might want to tell me about the robbery anyway so she went ahead and broke the ice for you." He smiled before taking a sip of his coffee.

"You could have led with that." She quirked an eyebrow.

"And miss this brooding side of you that wants to tell me something but isn't sure of the ethics of it? Never."

She relished his charming smile and realized it had been a while since she'd seen it. "Now that the cat's out of the bag, what do you think?"

"I think the waters are muddy."

When he didn't elaborate, she asked, "What does that mean?"

"It means I think there are too many cooks in the kitchen —or whatever other metaphor you want to use that says this stinks. First the string of cat burglaries in the area just before a mass of actors come to town and then threatening notes left for one of those stars. Now this? It's strange."

"Because the note doesn't fit."

"Exactly." Nelson shifted his gaze to the ocean behind Charlie. "It feels so dramatic. Why draw attention to Katherina like that?"

Charlie blinked at his casual use of her name. "Oh, do you know Ms. Kent?"

He chuckled. "We've met."

"I see."

His smile widened. "Not jealous, are you?"

"I've met her as well." She smiled back, just as widely, but caught the flicker of his gaze. She wasn't sure if he'd meant her responses to be jealousy of him and another woman, or jealousy of meeting the star.

"Either way, it would appear those things aren't connected, but it *is* a little coincidental," Nelson said.

"I was going to ask about any other robberies that may have been reported, but I really don't want to put myself on Ben's hit-list yet again."

"You and he need to kiss and make up," he said, then added, "not literally."

"If only it were that simple." She pushed thoughts of the grumpy security officer aside. "What have you been thinking with regards to all of this?"

"Why do you ask?" Nelson leaned forward, elbows on the small table.

"Because you're the kind of person who thinks about things like this—just like me. You're not someone who sits by and lets the police have all the fun."

He barked a laugh. "Well said. And you've got keen instincts, my dear. I was actually looking for you when I found you here."

"Why was that?"

"Because the night Ms. Kent got that note, I put out some feelers."

"What type of feelers?" Charlie knew that Nelson had been an investigator for the army before becoming a potter, and she'd guessed he'd done some of his own PI work, though she had no evidence to back that up yet. Either way, she wasn't surprised to learn he had sources and even less surprised that he'd reached out to them.

"I did hear back from a guy in Cuba who deals in gemstones." Nelson leaned closer. "He says that there has been chatter about a necklace that matches the description of Katherina's necklace."

"As in, it's already on the market? How can that be?"

"I'm not sure if it's truly for sale or just word that it *will* be is what he's talking about. I got this information through an encrypted email and have sent a follow-up but I don't expect to hear back right away."

"Can this source be trusted?"

Nelson smiled. "I pay well for actionable information and he knows that. If there is anything else for him to share, I'll know about it. It just depends on when."

"Where does that leave us?" Charlie leaned back, the last few sips of her drink turning to cold water as the ice melted.

"On the defensive, I suppose."

"There's no way to know *who* put out that info, I assume?"

"No." Nelson's answer was definitive. "But I'll keep looking into it. I would assume they have to get their hands on the necklace sometime between it leaving the hotel vault and when it's returned—unless there is an even more elaborate heist planned and they are going to break into the vault."

"That seems unlikely," Charlie said.

"I agree. So that means the window is narrow. That's a good thing as much as it is a difficult thing."

"Good because we know when that will be. Difficult because of *when* it will be."

"The premiere gala." He nodded. "I know. You'd think a thief would choose a different time, but that's when she was planning to wear the necklace, right?"

"From what I understand," Charlie admitted. "You don't think there's a chance she'd forgo wearing it, do you?"

"I don't know her well, but I'd guess not. Part of the allure of the gems, aside from their value, is the fact that it's a status symbol for her—in essence."

"If she doesn't have the necklace, it's less attention on her. I understand that."

They fell into silence for a few minutes. Charlie fell prey to her thoughts and wondered if it could be as simple as having Ben assign a guard to follow Ms. Kent whenever she went. Wouldn't that solve the issue?

She was about to voice that very thought when Nelson leaned back. "At least we have a few days to make a plan."

Charlie found herself nodding. "That's true. I was just thinking it would make the most sense to have a guard assigned to stick to her like glue."

"Would she go for that? It would distract from the cameras." Nelson shrugged.

"We could tell her to play it off as if he is the new man in her life." Charlie laughed. "You could volunteer?"

Nelson didn't join her laughter, and her breath caught at the back of her throat. The raw emotion on his face was clear—hurt. It couldn't be from her comment, though. She'd teased him in this manner before and he'd never reacted like this.

"Sorry. I-I shouldn't have said that."

"No. I know you were joking." He cleared his throat and ran a thumb along the ridge of his coffee cup. "I've been off lately. I'm sorry for that."

Charlie wanted to tell him she knew—and that she understood—but the moment passed as his grief ebbed and was replaced by a cunning expression. "I'll let you know when my source gets back to me and we'll come up with a plan for the premiere. There's got to be a way— even if it's a small tracker on the necklace—to keep it safe."

"Sounds like a plan," Charlie said.

They stood in tandem, and Nelson smiled down at her. "Thanks for the chat, Charlie. It's been too long since we've done this."

"What? Colluded on a case?" she said with a grin.

"Acted like friends." His expression turned serious but then he offered a wink before walking off.

She watched him go and replayed his words. They were friends, weren't they? Which meant she had every right to ask him about his wife and how he was doing. Why, then, did it feel so difficult when those hazel eyes were looking into hers?

IT WAS CASINO NIGHT, part of the lineup of events leading to the premiere, and Charlie found herself back in the borrowed black dress. She really needed to get a dress of her own, or perhaps a few, if these high-class nights were going to be typical for working at the resort, but for now, she was thankful black seemed to be the color for the night.

Everywhere she turned, men and women wore black and white in various styles. A white tuxedo, a black dress, a white dress, a black tuxedo, with occasional flashes of other colors—red, gold, purple.

"You look great. You really should just keep that dress," Valentina said. She had chosen a white, floor-length gown that hugged her generous curves and her hair was pulled back and twisted up with pearls dotting the curls that hung down. She looked like an elegant albino mermaid.

"I promise to get my own," Charlie vowed. "I was just thinking about that. I may need to if we're going to have so many events back to back."

"I know." Valentina nodded. "I realize it's all hands on deck right now, and usually I'm up for a good party, but I've been missing my home-time with Stephen. We've been watching a new crime documentary, and I can't wait to find out why the killer did it."

"Don't you mean who the killer is?" Charlie said.

"I think I already know, but I want to know why. There just doesn't seem to be a good motivation for him to have killed the woman he supposedly loved." Her gaze shifted to the sky as she appeared to consider all angles of the case, and Charlie laughed, stepping into her with a gentle elbow push.

"Come back to the party, Detective Lopez."

"I like the sound of that," Valentina said. "Then again, I don't want to have to wear those horrid pantsuits you see all the female detectives wearing. *Bor-ing.*" She broke the last word up as if it were two words and rolled her eyes for good measure.

They stood at the edge of the back garden area that abutted the private pool. Tonight, the gates had been opened to create a type of high-class outdoor party and round tables had been erected across the space.

Everywhere you turned, there was a casino game going. Guests played with tokens that didn't actually represent money, but they would be able to cash in their chips at the end of the night for prizes.

From what Charlie had gathered, each guest had paid a hefty sum to attend the night with the cast from *A Night of Starlight*. The proceeds were going to a charity that Katherina had chosen herself.

The salty scent of the ocean was on the breeze, and it had cooled down considerably once the sun began to set. Strategic fans and misters were placed in the garden and helped to add a cooling breeze, but Charlie thought the night was just right for a party.

"I love what Juliana did with the decorations," Valentia said.

Charlie nodded. "She really had an excellent vision for tonight and utilized the team well to get it done."

"Margery was bragging about how detailed Juliana was and how this was going to be the best coordinated party they'd had in a long time. She's so sorry she had to miss it."

Charlie's mind supplied the image of the event coordinator at the Pearl Sands. She was short and mousey with curly blonde hair, a pert nose, and reading glasses she always wore around her neck. While she looked to be in her mid-forties, Charlie thought she acted more like a librarian from the nineteen-forties with her clothing choices.

"Her staff has had a busy time this week. So many parties and events to plan." Charlie shook her head. "I thought it was bad enough coordinating the guest excursions and making sure everyone has everything they want and need, but that is a headache all its own. She'll be happy to know it seems to be going off without a hitch."

"Because of you," Valentina pointed out.

"Not really. We all came together. I had so much help and, like you said, it's all hands on deck this week."

The women fell into silence as music from a live four-piece band played across the gardened area. The quiet was interrupted by shouts of laughter, cries of dismay, and light chatter that filtered to them through the manicured grounds.

Everywhere Charlie looked, she caught sight of sparkling lights woven through tree branches and into bushes. The black-and-white theme had transferred to the tables.

"I feel like a chaperone at a high school dance," Valentina finally observed.

"We're here to ensure the guests' satisfaction and to see to their needs." Charlie spoke like she was reading from the resort manual.

Valentina groaned. "You sound like a female version of Felipe. Speaking of, where is he?"

"I'd been wondering the same thing. I saw him flitting around all day today, going from guest to guest like it's his personal goal to ensure everyone is having a good stay."

Charlie laughed. "I know it's his job, but I wanted to take a break just watching him."

"He pours all he has into this job."

Charlie nodded. She knew that there was also one other thing he poured his heart into, and that was his mother. He knew balancing his job with helping her settle into her new environment had been a lot for him. Charlie wasn't sure if he was too proud to ask for help or honestly didn't know how to, but it was one of the things that had softened Charlie toward him.

He was a lot to handle sometimes, with his hyper-fixation on the details of his job and making sure everyone was doing their absolute best, but at his core, she knew him to be a kind, patient man who wanted the best for those he cared about.

Thoughts of him reminded her that, once this week was over, they needed to sit down and have a serious conversation. Dread at the thought coiled around her midsection, but she pushed the thoughts aside. There was nothing she could do about that tonight, so there was no sense in taking on the worry.

The night wore on, and Charlie and Valentina were both called away at separate times to help with this detail or that, but they continued to come back to "their station," as Valentina had called it, near a flowing fountain that had a good view of the majority of the party.

Valentina had just been called away to help with something in the women's bathroom when Charlie felt a prickle against her neck. It felt like someone was watching her.

Working as a policewoman and as a PI, Charlie had learned to heed those feelings. As unobtrusively as possible, she turned to look behind and to the sides of her. Nothing was amiss. No one turned away when she shifted in their direction. No one was even looking at or even near her.

It was an odd sensation, but she trusted it and took a few steps forward. From her vantage, she could now see further into the party and caught sight of Gwyn in a stunning white gown with black at the tips of the ruffles. Next to her stood Elliot Armstrong and a few fans—at least that's who Charlie guessed them to be by the way they ogled him. He wore a white tux with a black tie and a red pocket square.

Beyond him, she caught sight of Raji in a black tux, black shirt, and black satin tie. He was chatting with a beautiful woman wearing an equally black dress and sipping from a glass of champagne. She looked familiar. Perhaps she'd been one of the people who'd checked in early with Katherina.

Just beyond them was Katherina, the belle of the ball. She was talking with Thornton Blackwell and another young man. She stood out in a black-and-white dress with edges of blood red and wore her blonde hair slicked back. It reminded Charlie a little of a Bond villain, and she had to hold back her smile.

When the star turned, Charlie caught her breath. There, around her neck on display for all to see, was *the necklace.*

Charlie took a step forward, but the next second, every light in the garden cut out.

Despite the resort lights still being on, the garden rested in the shadow of the eastern wall and any light she could see did nothing to aid in making the garden visible. They all had light blindness now that darkness had descended.

Screams and cries rang out, and Charlie heard questions about what had happened. Charlie was wondering the same thing when a scream rose above the rest. It was shrill and sounded somewhat familiar, followed by a clear cry.

"My necklace is gone!"

9

THE NEXT HALF-HOUR was controlled chaos on the grounds of the Pearl Sands. She and Valentina rushed off to help disoriented guests, some who had even tripped and fallen, and the rest who oscillated between fear and outrage.

As Charlie helped an older woman in a sleek black dress, her head spun at the reality of the threat against Katherina coming true, but she also had questions. She had just seen the woman and those who were close to her. Was it possible one of them had stolen it? Or, in a more complex theory, she wondered if it was possible that Katherina had taken her own necklace.

It was a wild theory, and one Charlie wasn't going to share outside of her own thoughts for the time being, but it was possible. Still, if that were the case, Katherina would have needed the help of someone else to cut the lights.

When they had come back on, everyone had shifted positions. Charlie hadn't gotten an accurate look on who was—or *wasn't*—around Katherina now.

Charlie blinked, realizing she'd been lost in thought while Sophia spoke. "What did you say?"

"I asked if you wanted to be there when I question Ms. Kent. Are you all right?" Sophia leaned close, peering into Charlie's eyes.

"I was thinking."

"About?"

Charlie stared back at the woman and was momentarily caught off guard by the dramatic change in their relationship. They had started off almost at odds and now they were... What? Friends? Perhaps something close to that.

"Yes, I'd like that."

"Oh, great," Sophia said.

Charlie followed her gaze and saw Ben Simmons walking their way. When the lights had finally come back on and Katherina's scream had shattered the night, security was quick to arrive. There had already been guards stationed at every entrance to the private event, but Ben had to have been observing the cameras, or someone in his office was, when the lights went out.

It made sense for him to be there, but even more so when the word of the theft had reached security personnel. As he drew near, Charlie saw someone else behind him and now wondered which person Sophia had been reacting to.

"Hello, Mr. Delgado," Sophia said. She dipped her head and pulled her shoulders back. She wore a royal blue blouse and black slacks with sensible black boots with a low heel. Her detective's badge was fastened to her belt opposite her gun. She looked every bit the imposing detective, even standing at 5'3".

"Detective Perez. What is going on?" Felipe's eyes were wide and seemed to be taking everything in at once—or trying to.

Charlie felt bad for the man. Since she'd come to the resort, it had been one thing after another, and yet each time, he'd seemed to handle things well—or as close to that as he could get. He was demanding though, in the way a resort manager had to be, and she expected to see that side of him come out tonight.

"I've just arrived on scene, really." Sophia looked to Charlie. "Charlie was filling me in on what had happened from an observer's standpoint, and Mr. Simmons just arrived so I was going to ask him what he observed from a security standpoint."

Ben's eyes narrowed as if he were searching for an untruth in her words, but he gave nothing else away. "I'm sorry to say my security office—and all our cameras—went dark along with the blackout here."

"But the rest of the resort remained lit," Charlie said.

"I suppose we were targeted as well." Ben turned to Felipe. "We need to cordon off this area and get Ms. Kent to a private room. And anyone else who was near her needs to be stopped. I think it would be best if—"

"It would be best if I was the one giving the directions." Sophia broke in with a weak smile. "I appreciate your quick thinking, but this is now the scene of a crime and we'll be investigating it as such."

"We will do everything we can to work in tandem with you, Detective Perez." Felipe's gaze shifted to Charlie. "You will act as liaison."

Charlie looked to Ben. She couldn't help the gut reaction, but all she saw was a quick flex of the man's jaw muscle. "Whatever is best for the resort."

"Where can my men be to be of the best use to you, detective?" Ben asked, as if Charlie hadn't spoken.

"Ms. Davis, I would like a word." Felipe's tone left no room for refusal.

"Find me when you're done," Sophia said before turning to speak with Ben.

Charlie followed Felipe a few paces away, and that was when she saw the crack in his façade. He was close to exploding with pent-up energy.

"Take a deep breath," she instructed.

He shot her a look. "I will not calm down, if that is what you are asking."

"Anger and decision-making don't mix well."

"Do you not think I know that?" he snapped.

"I'm sorry. How are you?"

He looked taken aback by her question. "I— This is horrible."

"I mean *you*." She let her hard look portray her thoughts.

"I spoke with Ms. Kent not but a few hours ago. I stood there and assured her that her priceless necklace would be safe on the grounds of the resort. And then this." He shook his head, a hand reaching up to rub across his mouth.

"You couldn't have known. And, in any other situation, it *would* have been safe." That was what had Charlie bothered. She, as well as others, had assumed—wrongly— that Katherina would be wearing the necklace for the premiere. Why else would she bring an expensive, custom necklace with her? But no, she'd worn it tonight and, by all accounts, it would appear that whoever stole it had known that. *How* had they known it?

"I do not know what will happen. I could lose my job."

"This isn't your fault, Felipe." Charlie resisted the urge to reach out and touch his arm. She would consider the resort manager a friend, but they were in the middle of a tense situation and she didn't want anyone to misconstrue her actions as anything more than kind support.

"It may not be, but someone will have to answer for this."

"The thief." Charlie met his gaze and flashed a reassuring smile. "Now, let me go liaise with Detective Perez and we'll see what can be done."

He nodded, his mouth shifting to a tight line. "I will speak with Ben."

Charlie watched him walk toward the security officer with a grim expression and saw Ben's responding hard features. She felt a lightbulb go off. She hadn't considered the fact that, while Felipe was responsible for the resort, Ben was responsible for the security of it and the guests. Was it possible he felt the pressure being in charge and yet so many things had gone wrong?

It gave her a different perspective of the man and softened some of her frustration with him. They were in a difficult situation, and everyone wanted what was best for the guests as well as the resort itself.

"You coming, Charlie?" Sophia asked.

She turned and followed the detective, who had just finished up a conversation with one of the security guards.

"Did you get any new information?" Charlie asked.

"Not really. He's young and, while observant, he can't see in the dark. No one can."

"So the lights remove any chance we'll get information from cameras, correct?"

"It's not even that, Charlie." Sophia lowered her voice. "The security feeds were cut."

"I know Ben said the power was out there, but isn't there a backup?"

"Gone too." Sophia shook her head. "I don't like it. It screams of prior planning, and yet when considering Ramona's incident, it doesn't fit."

Charlie had been thinking the same thing. Ramona's villa had been burgled when she was asleep, no breaking or entering visible, and no alteration of the cameras—or so Charlie assumed, since there had been no report of it.

They exited the garden area into a bland hallway used by resort staff and made their way toward the other end. "They said Katherina was placed in a free room at the end of this wing," Sophia explained.

Charlie nodded and followed along. The corridor ended in glass double-doors that opened into a small courtyard where room doors encircled the small space. Charlie had only been in this area a handful of times, but she knew each room was a wedge-shaped suite. The outer side created a type of circular tower that overlooked the beach. The bottom rooms had access to a path that led to the beach.

"Let me do the talking," Sophia said.

Charlie nodded. She wondered if Ms. Kent would recognize her from the first night when she'd found the threatening cards. As a celebrity, she probably met new people all the time, all vying for her attention. Charlie couldn't imagine that kind of lifestyle and was thankful she didn't have to.

Sophia knocked once, and a burly man opened the door. Sophia flashed her badge and he let them both in. Charlie didn't recognize him and wondered if he was private security hired by Ms. Kent. If so, where had he been during the party?

"Ms. Kent, I'm Detective Sophia Perez. I have a few questions to ask you." Sophia charged into the room without an ounce of hesitation. She wore her status as law enforcement with pride and directness, something Charlie appreciated about her. Her bluntness could also be seen as rudeness though, and Charlie hoped Katherina saw the professionalism more than the directness.

"Hello." Katherina sat in an armchair near a floor-to-ceiling sliding glass door covered in flowing white curtains. She still had her expensive gown on, but her shoes were gone, tossed to the side, and her neckline was shockingly bare. A stark reminder of why they were there.

Charlie noticed she still wore diamond stud earrings as well as a tennis bracelet and a gaudy diamond ring. So, not all of her jewelry had been taken. A necklace was much easier to lift than a ring, but it wasn't impossible for a truly good thief.

"I'm sorry for what you've experienced tonight, but I do have to ask these questions. Is that all right?"

"Yes." Katharina's gaze drifted to Charlie.

"This is Ms. Davis. She'll be assisting me tonight through her role at the hotel."

"The PI, right?"

She did remember. Charlie nodded.

Katharina's gaze settled back on the detective. "I don't mind. What do you need to know?"

Sophia pulled the second chair over so she could face Katherina, and Charlie took a seat on the bed. They made a kind of oblique triangle, but it worked best to see the woman's face. Charlie wouldn't be asking the questions, but she wasn't a casual observer. Sophia had asked her to come for a reason, and she thought it might just be something like this—to be a second set of eyes and ears.

"First of all, have you thought any more about who might have wanted to steal your necklace since you received the threat on those cards?"

"No." The star ran a hand over her hair, though it remained perfect. "Honestly, I thought that was a joke. I wouldn't have worn it tonight if I still thought there was a threat."

"Why would you think it a joke?"

"Because I'm at this lavish resort with security everywhere. Who would be foolish enough to try something?" Her words were cut off with a chocked sob. "I'm sorry. This shouldn't be so hard, it's not like anyone has died. I just...I didn't think it would happen. I thought it was a prank. Someone trying to throw me off or a weak grab for attention, but then no one claimed it so I thought it was done. I was wrong."

Charlie could follow the woman's logic. It made sense that she felt invulnerable to the point that she had risked wearing the necklace, but was she acting? Or were her tears genuine?

"What made you choose tonight to wear the necklace?" Sophia asked.

"I don't know." Katherina wiped under her eyes. "It looked good with this dress?"

"Were you not planning on wearing it to the premiere?" Sophia asked, channeling Charlie's thoughts from before.

"I hadn't really decided. I'm a bit of a free spirit when it comes to what I'll wear to events. Just ask Gwyn. I bring a *lot* of clothes with me when I travel so I have the freedom of choice. I'm a mood dresser, or so I call myself." She offered a polite laugh before sobering.

"Who did you tell that you were wearing it tonight?"

Charlie almost smiled at the question she would have asked as well, but she pulled her thoughts back to focus on how Katherina answered.

"Lars." She motioned to the man standing by the door. "I brought him on as my personal bodyguard. I'd asked about his availability at first and then after the incident with the cards, I thought he was necessary. He's very professional and well vetted. Aside from him, I think Gwyn knew. And of course the hotel manager."

Charlie's stomach clenched. Felipe knew she was wearing it that night, but had he added security measures? Charlie didn't want to think about what could come back on him if it was determined he had not taken every precaution he could. Would Katherina demand his job in payment of her loss? She didn't seem the type, but Charlie couldn't be certain.

"Anyone else? Think hard, Ms. Kent. This is a shift in your behavior, of no fault of your own, but it would mean that whoever did steal it tonight had foreknowledge."

That, or someone had bugged the phone in her room—or the room itself—when she called Felipe to arrange getting the necklace from the vault. Charlie knew the procedure for that was routine, but also secretive. No one wanted to announce they were going in to the vault to retrieve expensive items. It was a reason the vault had a private entrance and exit that only the guests were able to access.

"No one that I can think of. But...I don't know. Sometimes, I talk if I get tipsy. I may have mentioned something at dinner last night. That's when I'd made up my mind to wear it."

Charlie shared a look with Sophie. One night wasn't enough time to set up something like this, was it?

"I see." Sophia took some notes. "I'll need a list of everyone who was at that dinner."

"You don't think it's someone I know, do you?" Katherina appeared scandalized.

"We don't know yet, Ms. Kent. Best to cover all bases. Now, can you tell me what happened?"

Katherina described the scene as Charlie had remembered it. "And then the lights went out. Everyone was shocked. I heard screaming, and someone tripped and fell, I think. And I was jostled to the side. Thankfully, Thornton was there and caught me before the lights came back on. And that's when I realized the necklace was gone. My hand went up to my neck, force of habit when I wear such expensive jewelry, and it was gone. Just...gone."

"Did you feel anything?"

"No." Katherina was close to tears again. "I've been wracking my memory, trying to think of the moment I didn't feel the weight anymore, but there wasn't a time I can pinpoint."

"A skilled thief can be very talented when it comes to taking something off of us." Sophia flashed a knowing smile. "Don't be too hard on yourself. Now, you said that someone bumped into you. Was it a man or a woman?"

"I— I don't know."

"Did they say anything? Such as, 'excuse me' or 'pardon'?" Sophia pressed.

"No." Katherina was adamant. "I just felt Thornton's hand steadying me. I think I must have reached out to him when I was off balance."

"I see. Did you smell anything? Perfume? Cologne? Sometimes, when darkness takes out one of our senses, our other ones compensate."

"No, I'm sorry. I wish I could tell you something helpful, but I can't. Believe me, I would if I could."

"I understand. Is there anything else you think I should know? Any other threats in your life? Jealous exes? Anything at all that would make you the target of a jewel thief?"

"Nothing." Katherina said the word with finality. "I know there are scandals all the time in Hollywood, but I try my best to stay out of that—and out of the limelight. The most publicity I get is for movies and perhaps for the things I wear. As for threats, I don't get them like other stars do. I mean, yes, in the past, I've gotten a few overly zealous fan letters that skew creepy rather than supportive, but we've had each one looked into. It's why I have Lars on call, just in case something happens."

"And where were you, Mr.—"

"Lars Zondervan. I was standing about ten feet away, observing Ms. Kent from a distance as she prefers at parties like this." He stood tall, no hint of emotion or defensiveness on the rigid planes of his blocky face. There was no extra tension in the lines of his shoulders or the way his hands stayed open at his side. "When the lights went out, I did move to step forward, but someone got in my way and I was slightly delayed in reaching her."

Now Charlie saw his jaw clench. He was mad at himself for not being next to her.

"You had no way of knowing they were after the necklace," Katherina said encouragingly.

She was different than most stars Charlie had interacted with, and it strengthened her desire to find who had taken her necklace.

"I see. There wasn't much you could do without power." Sophia noted something else and then looked up, her expression curious. "I'm assuming people pulled out their phones for light?"

"It was a cellphone-free party tonight," Katherina explained before Charlie had the chance to. "Honestly, I loved the thought of it. I could go, enjoy the food, and talk to whoever I wanted to. I didn't have to worry about anyone taking a photo that I'd be shocked to see in the tabloids the next day."

"So there really was no light. When did you find out the party was going to be like that?"

"Months ago."

Sophia nodded. "Thank you for your time, Ms. Kent. I may need to question you again, but for now, I'm sorry for what you've lost and will do my best to uncover the person or persons behind the theft."

Katherina only nodded and slumped back against the cushioned chair, looking both elegant and defeated.

Charlie followed Sophia out of the suite and waited until they were out earshot. "You know what I'm thinking?"

"Probably something similar to what I am," Charlie said with a humorless smile.

"This was planned months ago."

Charlie nodded. "But how is that possible when even Katherina didn't think she was going to wear the necklace tonight?"

"That, Charlie, is the question we have to uncover. Find the answer to that and we'll find who stole Ms. Kent's diamond necklace."

10

It was a long night made longer still by the fact that Felipe expected to be filled in after their conversation with Katherina, but Charlie wasn't sure what she could share. She knew this was an open investigation, but she didn't know what would be pertinent and what would only make Felipe squirm from his lack of foresight.

As she approached the security office, she took in the familiar exterior. Stucco walls painted white with a sturdy, reinforced door and a small plaque that simply stated, "Security Office." Nothing to make the space stick out or draw attention. You could find it, but it was a place most guests would need to be led to.

She wondered how the thief could have found the power linked to this room specifically, as well as the garden. It showed a level of knowledge that shouldn't be available outside of the office itself, but she'd met some resourceful robbers in the past.

"There you are," Felipe said, coming up behind her. "We will meet in Ben's office."

Charlie held her tongue and followed him inside. The office was always cold—too cold—to protect and compensate for the additional electronics needed to keep an eye on the resort, but tonight, the chill seeped into Charlie's core.

She still wore Valentina's elegant dress and briefly wondered where her friend had gotten to. They'd parted ways to cover more ground as the disorder of the party grew, and then she'd gone off with Sophia. Charlie would have to text her later to make sure she'd made it home safely.

"Charlie?" Felipe looked down at her with concern.

"Long night. I'll be fine."

He looked unconvinced but pushed open the door to Ben's office without so much as a knock, motioning for her to take a seat. "Ben, I need answers."

Ben's gaze shifted to Charlie. "I'm sure she has more than I do."

The slight was so bold that all Charlie could do was stare.

"I was not asking about the necklace. I am concerned with the power failure and what that signifies for the Pearl Sands."

"I'm not sure that I have the answers you're looking for. We've got a guy on call who will be here soon, but I didn't tell him to rush since the power came back on."

"No rush?" Charlie had told herself to remain quiet until called on, but this was ridiculous. "You need to look into issues that deal with *your* office."

Felipe clenched his teeth. "She's right. We need to know what happened to see if there is going to be another robbery—or something even worse."

Ben looked on the verge of arguing but seemed to decide to bite his tongue. "I will."

Felipe leaned forward and placed a hand on Ben's desk. "I am tired of being behind on all of these things. I assured Ms. Kent that she and her property would be safe, and by all accounts, she should have been, and yet her high-value necklace goes missing. What am I supposed to think? What am I supposed to do?"

"I really think it's a matter for the police." Ben's reply seemed to be the wrong one.

"The police will do what they can. I am talking about the reputation of this resort. There is no way I can continue to feel confident hosting the events we have scheduled if we are at risk for another power outage or worse."

"Have there been other thefts?" Charlie spoke the question into the tense silence.

Both men turned to her, but it was Ben who spoke. "How did you know?"

144

"What?" Felipe's head snapped to the security officer.

"There was a report on my desk this morning from one of our guests saying that she can't find a specific piece of jewelry. I hadn't yet informed you because we're not sure if it is accurate or not."

"What does that mean?" Felipe demanded.

"She's traveling with an aide and has been known to be forgetful in the past. She likes to blame the maids, but I know each person who has had entry to the room and no one has been a red flag. It's more likely she misplaced the item."

"Or someone took the card of someone that wouldn't be flagged," Charlie added.

"I— There's no evidence of that."

"Which also means there is no evidence against that." Felipe ran a hand down his face. "I want it investigated. Charlie, look into it as well."

She saw Ben flinch out of the corner of her eye and was quick to protest. "I don't have to—"

"Please." Felipe met her gaze.

She was on the verge of telling them about Ramona, but something made her hold back. Ramona had all but begged for her theft not to be shared, and Charlie would continue to honor that since at the very least, Sophia knew.

"I'll see what I can do."

"This is ridiculous," Ben groused.

"Do you have something to share?" Felipe's tone was cool and even.

"She is—*was*—a private investigator. Nothing more. It's not like she's police, and I've worked this job for five years. Why are we having her involved?"

"Because she is my secret weapon."

Both Charlie and Ben swiveled to look at him.

"What?" Charlie asked.

"Ben is on the resort website as the head of security. He works in this office, wears a security shirt, and does security things. You, Charlie, are not that. You interact with guests, you are free do go where you need to, and you have a job that necessitates you speaking often with guests of all kinds. Who better to gain true insight into the lives of our guests than a concierge?"

"She's a spy?" Ben's words sounded like an eyeroll.

"She is undercover, in a sense, and that is important to the Pearl Sands."

Charlie hadn't seen it that way. Not at first, at least, but as Felipe explained his reasoning, she could concede that it made some sense. With her background, she had legitimate experience to question people the right way, but from her current position, she also had the means to do what she needed to around the resort.

"I'm not here to take your job, Ben." She spoke the words she thought he wanted to hear the most. "I don't want to be head of security—or in the security office at all. I like what I do, though sometimes I find myself slipping into my past life as a PI. Why can't we work together?"

Ben's eyes narrowed. "I hadn't seen it that way, Felipe." He shifted to look at their boss. "I'll do my best to share information with Ms. Davis when it is needed."

She knew that, for Ben, that was a much a sign of capitulation as she was going to get. "I'll take it."

They held each other's gaze for a moment in a way that felt a little like a truce, and then Felipe slapped his knees with his palms.

"Good. See that you do. And keep me updated. I have to go." He stood to leave but speared them both with a look. "I don't want to see something else happen during this event week. I cannot afford it. The Pearl Sands cannot either."

CHARLIE HADN'T EXPECTED the knock on her door early the next morning. In fact, she'd only been awake for a half-hour when it came, and part of her hoped she was still asleep and dreaming.

When she opened the door and saw Valentina, Stephen, Nelson, *and* Ramona, she blinked any leftover sleep from her eyes and welcomed them inside. Better to accept reality than fight it.

"Am I missing something?" She stifled a yawn.

"Breakfast?" Valentina handed over a brown bag, and Stephen followed it up with a paper cup.

She opened it up to find a raisin bran muffin and took a big bite. Nelson sidestepped her to pull the chairs from her small, round kitchen table into the living area space so they could all sit facing one another. When that was done, they each took seats and Charlie asked, "Who's going to fill me in first?"

"It's about last night," Nelson began. "I heard through the grapevine what happened and, after Ramona shared with us her story, I think we all need to put our heads together. A meeting of the minds, if you will."

"Is this the crime club in action again?" Charlie couldn't help her smile.

"Crime club?" Nelson looked to the rest of the group as realization dawned. "You're going to have a club about crime without me?"

"Not necessarily," Valentina said. "We just hadn't gotten to a full meeting yet."

"I expect an invitation." Nelson did his best to look haughty.

"You're invited," Charlie said. "Now why are you all here?"

"We want to help you, Charlie," Stephen said.

His hopeful expression caused warmth to pool in Charlie's midsection. She met Nelson's gaze this time and he offered an encouraging nod. He might not have come as part of the club—yet—but he was there for her nonetheless. She could just imagine Valentina calling him up and asking him to join them in offering assistance. She guessed he hadn't hesitated one bit.

"All right. Then let me tell you what I remember—then you next, Valentina. Maybe there's something I've missed." Charlie jumped into describing the scene from last night and who she'd seen near or close to Katherina before the lights went out.

"Basically, all the people you'd expect to be in her sphere," Ramona said. She wore bright purple joggers and a high-end t-shirt that had "queen" written across the front.

"Yes, everyone except for the young man talking with Katherina and Thornton and the woman with Raji nearby," Charlie said.

"I think I know the young woman you're talking about. Her name is Scarlett Watkins. She's a well-known makeup artists from Hollywood—or so the rumors say. The young man doesn't sound familiar, though." Valentina looked to the rest of the group for help.

"I think that was Hank," Ramona added. Her eyes searched the ceiling as if she were filtering through her memories. "Yes, it would make the most sense if it were him. Can you describe him?"

"Tall, brown hair but with lots of blond highlights, and a chiseled jaw but a crooked nose," Charlie said.

"Dark-rimmed glasses?" Ramona narrowed her eyes.

"Yes."

"Then that's Hank. He's an up-and-coming director who worked a little on *A Night of Starlight* but just to get his feet wet. He's got a big production coming up, and I hear he's on the search for a star for it."

"Katherina?" Valentina exclaimed like the fan she was.

"She's one of the people he's interested in, so the gossip mill says. I've also heard that he's interested in making a name for himself, not just riding on the coattails of a well-known star." Ramona gave an elegant shrug.

"So he could be open to a lesser-known actresses," Charlie mused.

"It's possible."

"What is it you're thinking?" Nelson asked.

Charlie met his gaze and almost let her grin spread at the knowing look she saw reflected in his eyes. He understood that she was onto something.

"I spoke with Thornton a few days ago and he'd mentioned that he thinks Gwyn is only with Katherina for what it will do for her career. Since she was able to attend a party like we had here last night, I would say it's not out of the realm of possibility she is looking to rub shoulders with the *right people* while she works for Katherina."

"That doesn't seem earth-shattering, Charlie. No offense," Valentina said.

"True, but it was more than that. It goes back to wondering what was accomplished by the note. Did it make Katherina look slightly unstable, perhaps? Was it a way to—very subtly—discredit her in the eyes of the media and those in attendance at the gala?"

"And then her necklace is gone so she is in the light of the press more," Stephen added. "You would think, from the standpoint of a star, that's a good thing because any publicity is good publicity—or so they say. But if this new director wants low-key actors, then it could be bad."

"Good point, babe." Valentina squeezed his hand.

"How does this get us to *where* the necklace is?" Ramona asked.

"It goes back to the why. Did someone take the necklace for monetary value or is there a bigger picture?" Charlie popped the last bite of the muffin into her mouth, savoring the tart sweetness of the raisins against the dense bran texture.

"I've still got a call in to my contact in Cuba." Nelson looked around the room. "If the necklace is going to exchange hands, that would be the first place to look to find out *who* might be bringing it to sale."

"Money has to be part of it either way, right?" Ramona asked.

"You'd think so." Charlie leaned back. "Unless it's both."

"What does that mean?" Valentina asked.

"Money and position?" Stephen said.

"I'm not sure," Charlie admitted. "I just think we're not seeing something here."

"Then the question remains, what can we do to help you?" Ramona clasped her hands around her knee.

"I can talk with the maids and service workers who were there last night. Maybe someone saw something we didn't?" Valentina shrugged.

"And I'll do some online research into the key players here. I know tabloids and fan magazines aren't to be trusted, but there are some online sites that may have some celebrity gossip that is helpful." Stephen looked to Charlie for approval.

"Perfect. And, Nelson, you'll let us know what your contact says, right?"

He nodded.

"Then *I* will take the hard task of going out to lunch with our starlet." Ramona grinned. "She may open up to me about how this is affecting her—if at all—which would be helpful to know."

"Good idea, Ramona," Charlie said. "I'll continue to check in with those we saw near Katherina. If I can get a meeting with Mr. Chambers, I will as well, though I don't know if he's staying here or only coming for the events."

"He's here," Ramona supplied. "In a suite somewhere, I'm sure."

"Perfect." Charlie took a deep breath and blew it out. "I'll also check in with Sophia—um, Detective Perez. I'm sure there are things on her end that will help us as well."

"You think she'll share?" Valentina asked.

"We'll find out." Charlie grinned. "I hereby end this meeting of the Pearl Sands Crime Club."

They all burst into laughter, but it didn't affect the dedication she knew they'd each bring to their appointed tasks. Charlie had a feeling that one of them, if not all, would be crucial in finding who had taken the necklace and why.

11

CHARLIE'S DAY was filled with short meetings both in person and online to help families planning trips to the Pearl Sands as well as those already at the resort. Juliana had the morning off, but Charlie was surprised at the amount of work she'd gotten done in the shift she'd had before her.

Smiling as she went about scheduling a yacht excursion for a newlywed couple, Charlie almost didn't notice the shadow that passed across her desk.

"Good morning, Ms. Davis."

She looked up and smiled at Felipe. "Morning, Mr. Delgado."

There were dark half-moons under his eyes, and the crow's feet appeared more pronounced. She wondered if he'd gotten a call from the hotel owner—someone she'd never met—about what had happened.

"Is there anything to report?" His voice was pitched low, but she heard the tension in it.

"Not quite yet." She wanted to share with him that there was a group working on it, but she didn't want to give him cause to wonder if Valentina could complete her work duties or to worry about Ramona, a guest, being involved. She also knew how he felt about Nelson, though not why, so she kept that information to herself.

"I was going to speak with Mr. Armstrong on my break."

"Good. Yes. *Bueno*."

"Is there anything else I can do for you, Felipe?" She said his name softly, but she wanted to make sure he knew she was there if he needed someone to talk to.

Felipe had a weighty responsibility on his shoulders dealing with the resort, its guests, and everyone else under his direction, and she knew he took it very personally. There were sub-managers and people helping him at every turn, but he took a vested interest in anything that could reflect poorly on the resort.

"No. But thank you. There are fires to put out, as it were, but that is my responsibility. Please let me know the moment you have any more information."

"I will," she assured him.

He dipped his head and she returned to work, but his check-in had made her even more conscious of the fact she needed to get to the bottom of this. Not just for

Felipe, but for Ramona, Katherina, and the Pearl Sands as a whole.

The rest of the morning flew past in a blur of expensive excursions, dinner reservations at exclusive restaurants, and innocuous questions from patrons. She put up the ornate "be back soon" sign at the edge of her desk and headed to the staff breakroom.

There were only a handful of people there, and they were all gossiping about what had happened the night before. There was a lot of people saying they'd heard one thing or the other, but having been there herself, Charlie knew the rumors to be untrue.

She made herself a coffee and bought a prepackaged sandwich from the vending machine before leaving for a small courtyard where the staff could spend time on their breaks. It was hot and humid, but fans spun air downward and misters kept the worst of the heat at bay.

While the bread was a little stiff from being cold, the sandwich wasn't as bad as she'd expected and Charlie finished it quickly along with the hot coffee she'd gotten. She tossed her trash away and then, after double-checking for crumbs on her uniform shirt, she went to walk around the pool area.

Wandering around a crowded and popular area wasn't the most efficient way of finding someone, and Charlie didn't expect to see Elliot right away—or at all—but she always liked to check the pool areas first. That, and she wanted to get in some steps to negate all of the sitting she'd done that morning.

On the final lap of the second pool, Charlie sent a text message to Ramona, who immediately called her back.

"Hello, dear. Looking for Elliot?"

"Yes." Charlie held back a laugh. "Do you have any idea where he may be?"

There was muffled chatter on the other end of the line before Ramona came back on. "I'm here with Raji and a few others."

"Not more poker," Charlie joked.

"You know I can't resist a good game, and Raji is cleaning me out. I think he was hiding some of his talent." She laughed and said something away from the mic before coming back. "He says the last he heard, Elliot was going to the beach. He suggests looking somewhere remote. He likes to get away from it all. What's that?"

Charlie sensed that Ramona had moved the phone away again while she spoke with the young man.

"And he says to bring a peace offering. He likes the fruity drinks." Ramona let out a laugh. "No, you don't, you scoundrel!"

"What?" Charlie said.

"Sorry. That was about the game. Got to go. Bye!"

She hung up, leaving Charlie's mind reeling. At least she had an idea where Elliot was now. It seemed she would be heading to the beach.

Charlie took a moment to stop by her cottage and change out her work shoes for a pair of sandals before she walked toward the sand. She made one more stop at a bar on the beach, getting a fruity drink as Raji had advised, and then set off for a secluded area.

It felt good to slip out of the sandals and dig her toes into the sand, though the sun beating down made the task of walking toward the water less enjoyable.

Sweat trickled down her neck from beneath her blunt-cut hair just above her shoulders, but thankfully, her shirt was black and would hide the worst of it. By the time she reached the water, the spray had cooled the air somewhat.

She walked along the coastline toward the southern tip of the island where the residential stretch began but stopped a few hundred feet before where she saw the beach umbrella setup that Ramona had texted her about.

There, laying on a towel under a blue-and-yellow beach umbrella, Elliot lay prone with hands on his chest. There was a cooler, a few scattered books and a bag, and a sheet that hung down one side of the umbrella to effectively cut him off from the rest of the beach. She assumed that was on purpose.

She couldn't tell from this distance if he was sleeping, but her time was short and she'd rather apologize than ask permission.

"Mr. Armstrong, is that you?" Charlie shuffled up the beach toward him.

He sat up, pushing his sunglasses up into his hair, and flashed a questioning smile. He was wearing red boardshorts and no shirt. He was tanned and muscled and looked every bit the movie star.

"Uh, you'll have to remind me of your name. I'm sorry."

"Charlie Davis. I work for the resort." She stepped close to the shade of his umbrella. "I was actually looking for you. I was told to bring a fruity drink." She held it out to him.

He backed away from it. "Is there alcohol in that?"

Charlie blinked. "Yes, is that a problem?"

"I'm actually allergic."

"You are?" She set the drink down far away from him. "I'm sorry. I didn't know."

"I love the drinks, just can't have any alcohol in them."

Charlie nodded and wished Raji would have mentioned that. "Sorry about that, but do you have a moment to talk a little about what happened last night?"

His confusion deepened. "Last night?"

"When Ms. Kent's necklace went missing."

"I... Yeah. I guess?" He pulled on his shirt and crossed his legs. "Did you want to sit?"

He motioned to the beach chair that had a backpack in it, and she nodded. He pulled the pack off, and she took the seat, grateful for the shade.

"I'm sorry to bother you and I wouldn't under different circumstances, but I'm looking into the disappearance of Ms. Kent's jewelry as well as the odd happenings of late."

"You mean the cards."

"Yes."

"Can I ask why *you* are doing this? Isn't this a job for the police? Or hotel security?"

"Actually, I'm a private investigator and happen to work as a concierge. I get pulled into this a lot." Even as she said it, the words rang a little too true. She had done a lot of work for Felipe and, while she understood his reasoning behind having her investigate as he'd explained to Ben, it wasn't what she'd agreed to at the beginning.

"Once a PI, always one?" Elliot asked. His grin widened and he leaned back on his hand, tipping his head toward the ice chest. "Want a water?"

"No, thank you." Charlie mentally ran through the questions she wanted to ask. "Is there anything you can tell me from what you remember about last night? I know you've likely already told the police, but it would help me get a better picture of what happened."

He took a moment, his forehead scrunching in thought. "I don't really remember much. I was talking with a few people, and I remember thinking I wished it was over." He gave a humorless chuckle. "Premiere week is a lot of fun, but it's also a lot of work. I say work, but what I really mean is schmoozing."

"I can imagine it takes a toll."

"Why do you think I'm all the way over here?" This laugh was a little more genuine. "I had to wear a disguise to get past everyone on the beach and then set this all up." He gestured to the sheet that concealed him from view.

"And here I came to ruin your privacy. I'm sorry about that."

"It's okay. I get that you've got a job to do. But yeah, I don't remember much more than boring conversations about the film and not having my phone to distract me." He rolled his eyes. "Then I remember the lights going out. It was a shock with how dark it was. After that, it was all just Katherina's screams about her necklace and lot of confusion."

It sounded similar to what she had experienced. "Do you know anyone who would want to steal from Katherina?"

It was a broad question, but Charlie hoped that it might ignite conversation.

"I mean, plenty of people, I'm sure, but if you meant anyone who was at the party…" He looked off to the ocean for several minutes before answering. "I'd put my money on Gwyn."

Charlie's eyebrows rose at his definitive answer. "Really? Why?"

"She was supposed to be there last night as a type of moral support for Kat. That woman is a legend, but she gets social anxiety like you wouldn't believe. She never lets on, but those who know her can see it. Gwyn is kind of there in case Kat needs to get away or talk with someone familiar or something like that."

"But she wasn't doing her job," Charlie guessed.

"Not really. I mean, while in public Kat isn't going to out herself and demand she stay nearby in case Gwyn's needed, but that's my understanding of what Gwyn is supposed to do in those situations. Otherwise, she wouldn't have an invite, I don't think."

"But your friend Raji was there."

"Yeah, I guess, but he's more like a platonic plus-one." Elliot laughed and shook his head. "He's been there for me this last year—my craziest yet—and I feel it's literally the least I could do to bring him to events like this. We just get to hang out, catch up, stuff like that."

"Catch up?"

"Yeah, we knew each other as kids and then he had to move away. Stayed in touch a little through the years, but then he came back into my life at the perfect time."

"How so?" Charlie loved the sound of their friendship. Being the type of lone wolf that she was, their closeness since childhood was an enigma to her. One she wished she could personally understand.

"I'd just gotten the part in *A Night of Starlight*. You might have heard how my career blew up through social media. I'd done a few commercials and a smaller role in a movie, but this was big time. I felt in over my head, like I wasn't ready. Raji showed up and helped me ride the wave of fame—if you'll let me be poetic."

"I love that."

He nodded. "But, back to our question. When compared to how I treat Raji, Gwyn is most definitely Kat's assistant and gofer—not friend."

"I see." Charlie nodded.

"But last night, all she did was scope out directors and try to get into their good graces." Elliot made a disgusted face. "It's stuff like that *I* just won't do. I have standards. And I know that sounds snobby, but I feel like Gwyn is the type of person who will go out of her way to get what she wants—no matter the cost—and I'd decided when I first got into filmmaking, I was going to stay true to myself as much as possible."

He leaned back on both arms now, and Charlie thought she saw the young man more clearly. Sure, he was handsome in a way that Hollywood ate up, yet when he could be out being adored by young women in bikinis, he was hiding at the south end of the beach.

Still, his emphasis on Gwyn seemed a little too certain.

"Who is Gwyn to you?" she finally asked.

"No one." He said it flippantly, but she saw through the answer.

"In other words, you asked her out and she turned you down."

Charlie had been too blunt. She knew that the moment the words slipped from her lips, but she didn't take them back.

Elliot laughed. "You *are* a PI. That was intuitive, for sure. And yeah, you're not far from the truth there. We actually went to coffee once, a few weeks after she started working for Kat, but that was it. She ignored my requests for dinner, and I got the hint. I'm not bitter, if that's what you're getting at."

"I'm only getting at the truth, Mr. Armstrong."

"Call me Elliot." His smile widened. "Would *you* want to go to dinner with me?"

Charlie laughed, a blush creeping up her neck. "I'm well over twice your age, Mr. Armstrong."

He merely winked. "I live in Hollywood. Stranger things have happened."

"As flattering as that is, I'll need to pass."

"There's someone else, isn't there?" His attention narrowed in on her in a way that made her slightly uncomfortable. He saw through her protestations, but she could honestly say there wasn't anyone. Not at the moment.

"Not really." An image of Nelson flashed across her mind's eye.

"Sure, sure. Just tell me there is so my ego can recover."

She laughed now. "You're a hopeless flirt, and you certainly don't need me to stroke your ego, but I need to get back to work. Thank you for answering my questions."

She stood, but as she did so, the backpack he'd propped up against the beach chair fell forward and a few brochures fell out. She stooped down to put them back, but her attention snagged on one.

"Ziplining in...Cuba?" She held it up.

"I'm looking at my options for vacation." He quickly took the rest of the pamphlets from her and stuffed them back in his bag before bending to pull his shirt off again. "See you around, *Charlie*."

The wink was implied in his voice, and she merely smiled back before leaving, but his actions stood out to her.

Had he not wanted her to see brochures? And why not? Was it possible Elliot was hiding more than just a hurt ego from Gwyn? And if so, did it have anything to do with Katherina and her stolen necklace?

———

CHARLIE'S PHONE chimed as she left Elliot to lay back down enjoying a quiet moment to himself. She pulled her phone out and saw it was a message from Ramona to call her. One of several the woman had sent over the last fifteen minutes.

She pressed the call button, and Ramona picked up on the first ring. "Charlie."

"Sorry, I was talking with Elliot."

"I know, but I'd hoped you would answer anyway." Ramona took a breath. "There's been another theft."

Charlie stopped walking, toes in the sand. "What? Where?"

"Katherina again. The rest of her jewels are missing." She paused a beat. "From the *vault*."

Charlie bit her lip. How was this possible?

"You'd better come to her suite. She's not doing well and threatening to leave the resort. Felipe is here too, and I think he's shellshocked or something."

"I'll be right there." She confirmed the location of Katherina's suite and hurried across the sandy beach. The heat was sweltering, and she craved the cooling mist from the water as she trekked across the beach for a faster way toward the suites. She wouldn't have time to go back to her room for her closed-toe shoes, but she hoped that Felipe would forgive the oversight.

By the time she'd reached Katherina's door, Charlie was a sweaty mess. She diverted to a public restroom and wiped away the moisture from her face and neck, thankful for the air-conditioning in the bathroom, and then she rushed to the suite.

As if sensing her, Ramona opened the door and beckoned her inside. "Katherina is in there talking with Felipe and Lars. I told her you were coming, and she said it was fine."

"Good work," Charlie replied.

The woman, eccentric as she was, blushed with pride. "I'm selfishly hoping we can solve this and get *all* of our jewelry back."

"Me too." Charlie smoothed a hand over her shirt and stepped into the room.

"Ah, Charlie." Felipe sent her a look that begged for help, and she felt sorry for the added stress this was for him during an already stressful week.

Lars eyed her but didn't say anything as she took the proffered chair and faced Katherina Kent. "Ms. Kent, can you tell me what happened?"

"I called up to the hotel staff to access the vault. I thought that perhaps I'd just wear a less expensive set of gems to the cast special dinner tonight. I wanted to see what I had brought—I'd forgotten what we packed—but when I got there, they were gone."

"All of them?"

"Yes." Tears shone at the corners of Ms. Kent's eyes. "And what's worse is the attendant said a young woman had already taken them out for me."

Charlie's mind flashed to Gwyn. "Do you know anything about that?"

"Of course not." She looked indignant but then took a calming breath. "I did authorize Gwyn to have access to the vault with a key, but now I can't find her, and I can only think that she's stolen everything from me and taken off."

It was dramatic, but Charlie could see where the woman was coming from. "Is there footage?" she asked Felipe.

"Yes. It looks like Gwyn, though we can't get a good look at her face."

Charlie frowned. "And you don't know where Gwyn is?"

"I've tried calling, texting, even using the location finder—we share locations sometimes so we can find each other on larger sets—but I've got nothing. She must have turned her phone off. It's like she's dropped off the face of the earth."

Charlie took a measured breath. Two people had now pointed the finger at Gwyn, with a third making the same suggestion, and now this. Was it possible she was what everyone said?

There was something that nagged at the back of Charlie's mind, though. Something that didn't sit right with all of the evidence piling up against Gwyn.

"Do you know where Gwyn is *supposed* to be right now?"

The question seemed to take Katherina by surprise. "I—Uh, let me see." She pulled out her phone and swiped through a few screens until she came to what looked like a calendar app.

"I guess she's supposed to be free this morning. I mean, I do remember her requesting this morning off. Do you think she did that so she could rob me blind?"

Charlie offered a kind smile. "I don't think that's what's happening here." She couldn't put her finger on it exactly, but she had a feeling she was beginning to see the shape of things despite the fact there were still many gaping holes.

One memory came back to her: Gwyn nowhere near Katherina when her necklace was stolen. It was possible she was working with someone who *had* been close enough to take the jewelry, but Charlie was fairly positive it couldn't have been Gwyn who took it at the party.

Charlie's mind slowed. There was something in the memory-picture that drew her attention. Something that wasn't quite right, but she didn't know what it was.

A knock on the door drew everyone's attention, and Ramona opened it to show in Detective Perez. She took one look at Charlie and motioned for her. "Can I speak with you outside for one moment? Then I'll come and take your statement, Ms. Kent."

"Yes, of course." Katherina slumped back against her chair, head resting on a raised hand. She looked utterly defeated, and Charlie felt bad for the woman who had seen only loss since coming to the Pearl Sands.

Charlie stepped outside and quickly filled the detective in on what she'd come to learn.

"And what do you think?" she asked.

"I think it doesn't make any sense that Gwyn, who apparently has a key to the vault, would wait until a party to steal the most valuable necklace her boss has and then, the next day, take the rest out of the vault."

"Why not take them all from the vault to being with and leave the premises?"

"Exactly." Charlie nodded. The detective had come to her same conclusion. It didn't make sense.

"You think someone is framing Gwyn."

"It seems possible." Charlie wasn't sure who, though. Elliot? Katherina herself? Thornton Blackwell? There were too many players—and yet too few. Whoever had been on the security footage looked like Gwyn. That had to be taken into account.

"I've got to get in there, but keep your ears open. I have a feeling there are connections we're missing."

"I agree." Charlie watched the detective walk back into the room before heading down the corridor toward the lobby.

She wondered, not for the first time, where Gwyn might be. The fact that she'd specifically asked for the day off made Charlie think that there was something else going on with her. Charlie's conversation with Elliot came back to her and inspiration struck. Wherever Gwyn was, she was doing something she wanted to hide from Katherina.

Something that likely *wasn't* the theft of her gems.

Charlie shifted directions and pulled out her phone. After a quick conversation with Elijah at the front desk, she diverted to the suites on the other side of the resort.

Knocking, Charlie held her breath and waited. A young man with big, round glasses opened the door a few minutes later. He looked at her quizzically, and she wondered if she had the wrong room. "Is Mr. Chambers in?"

His expression cleared. "Oh, no. He had a meeting. I'm his assistant. Can I help you with something?"

"I've got an urgent matter to bring to him. You don't happen to know where he's taking this meeting, do you?"

The assistant hesitated then pulled out his phone. "He does have another room in the hotel where he's been taking appointments, but he books it under a different name." The man rattled off the number and shrugged. "Maybe don't tell him I gave it to you?"

She smiled reassuringly at him. "I won't. And thank you."

Room number in hand, Charlie made her way through the maze of corridors toward the wing where she thought this room was. Unlike the maids who knew the resort maze like the back of their hands, she was still unfamiliar with a few sections. It took her longer than she wanted to find the room.

At her knock, the sound of something crashing to the floor made her blood pulse faster in her veins. What was going on in there?

She knocked again, this time more insistently, and called out, "Hotel staff."

"Coming," a gruff voice said.

When the door finally opened, Charlie had to blink a few times to take in what she was seeing. Gwyn stood a few feet behind a shirtless Hank Chambers, her hair mussed and wearing a white robe. It was clear Charlie had interrupted something, but not as clear as the shame she saw on the young woman's features.

"Gwyn, the police need to speak with you."

Gwyn went white as a sheet. "What? Why?"

"They say you've stolen Katherina's jewelry that was held in the vault and have been trying to get a hold of you." Charlie ran her attention over Hank's face then turned back to Gwyn. "Best to get dressed. It's going to be a long afternoon."

12

CHARLIE STOOD and looked through the one-way glass. Gwyn sat huddled at an empty metal table. She wore a baggy t-shirt and leggings, much different from her stylish outfits when working for Katherina.

Sophia came up to Charlie and held out a cup of coffee. It was late, and Charlie usually didn't drink caffeine in the evening, but she accepted the warm liquid and took a sip anyway. It was bitter and cut with just a little cream.

"Glad you found her, but her story isn't making sense."

Charlie had overheard the first conversation the detective had with the young woman, but she knew that Sophia would go back in and ask for her to tell her story again. That's what Charlie had wanted to be there for. Sophia had—surprisingly—agreed.

"Do you want to come in?"

Charlie's eyes widened. "Can I?"

"Why not?" Sophia chuckled in a very uncharacteristic way. "As I told you, I'm only taking this case as a favor to another detective in the department, and I could use all the help I can get. I'm more homicide-focused, though I've worked burglaries in the past. Nothing to this extent, though."

"Then let's go." Charlie followed Sophia into the cold, square room.

Gwyn shifted back, her eyes going wide with apprehension.

"You know Ms. Davis here," Sophia began. "I'm going to let her sit in on this since she was the one to find you and has a bit of a vested interest in this case."

Gwyn didn't speak. She'd been asked if she wanted a lawyer, but she had declined.

"I've got nothing to hide. I'm happy to talk."

"Good. Then start again by going over what happened."

"Yes. Sure. Okay." She ran a hand through her hair and it fell over her shoulders in a fiery cascade. "I mean, it's no secret I want to get into acting. I'm only an assistant so I can get my foot in the door."

"Did Katherina know that when you started working for her?" Charlie asked. She hoped Sophia didn't mind her cutting in so early in the questioning.

"Not exactly. I mean, I didn't come out and tell my boss I was only working for her for what I could get out of it, but it's Hollywood. That's what's expected."

"Go on," Sophia said. She was taking notes but kept her gaze on the young woman more often than her notepad.

"It was the night the necklace went missing. That's when I finally met Hank Chambers." She flushed. "I saw it as my chance—had to shoot my shot, you know? I got a meeting with him and made sure to block myself off on Katherina's calendar." Gwyn's cheeks turned pink.

Meeting. Charlie was fairly certain that wasn't what she'd interrupted, but she didn't want to make the young woman feel uncomfortable. Instead, she asked, "Who has access to that calendar?"

"Me, Katherina, and Mr. Blackwell. Maybe Lars, now? I think that's it? I mean, sometimes when she's working on a movie, we'll get calendar invites and that kind of links to all our schedules, but that's only external appointments, not, like, someone *in* her calendar."

Sophia nodded. "So they knew you were going to be off duty, but you turned off your phone. Is that unusual?"

Gwyn's cheeks turned a deeper color. "Katherina is… demanding. She's a great actress, and I really look up to her, but as a boss, she can be a lot. I mean, she makes me turn on location-sharing sometimes. I don't even do that for my mom."

"You didn't want her to know where you were," Charlie summarized.

"Right."

"Because you were meeting with a director Katherina wanted to work with," Sophia added, consulting her notes.

"I wouldn't say it like that." Gwyn pushed a strand of hair behind her ear.

"Tell us about the key to the vault."

"I've already told you all of this. Before I turned off my phone, Katherina texted me and asked where I'd put my key because she'd lost hers. I told her, turned off my phone, and that was it."

"You're telling us that you didn't make a detour to the vault, take out all of Katherina's jewels, and then go meet with a director she's been hoping to work with? You're saying this isn't you?"

Sophia pulled out her tablet and turned it toward the young woman. A grainy image showed what Charlie would have guessed was Gwyn's back as she walked into the vault.

"Wh— That's not me."

"Where are the jewels, Gwyn? Stop lying to us."

Charlie shot Sophia a look. She'd gone from calm and collected to hard-nosed in less than a minute. Charlie knew some of the tactics from her time as a New York

City cop and her friendship with one of the detectives there, but she hadn't been prepared for this.

"I'm not lying. That is *not* me. I swear to you, I didn't take anything. Check Katherina's phone. You'll see the messages. I mean, seriously, why would I do that? Why ruin my career by stealing her gems if I was about to get the part she wanted?"

Why, indeed?

Charlie thought back through her conversation with Katherina. She hadn't mentioned a text message from Gwyn.

"Perhaps you wanted to add salt to the wounds," Sophia said. "If you really were going to get the part your boss wanted, why not have her gems too?"

"What would I do with them? I couldn't sell them, I'm sure they are marked or something. And why do it while I was here? There are so many other ways I could have stolen from Katherina that wouldn't have put me in the spotlight. I would guess a smart criminal would think of that."

"They would." Sophia's point was clear. If it were Gwyn, she wasn't being smart.

Charlie had to agree with the young woman, though. Their accusations didn't make sense—not in the grand scheme of things.

So who would have been able to gain access to the key and to looking like Gwyn?

"Does Katherina have a code on her phone?"

Gwyn blinked at Charlie's abrupt question. "What?"

"A passcode. Is it facial recognition or numbers or what?"

"I… It's both. There's facial recognition, but she's also got a code so that I can access it if I need to."

"Are you the only one who knows the code?" Charlie had an idea

"Yes. Well, no." She frowned. "I remember we all joked about it once, because Katherina was really tipsy one night after filming and most of the stars were there. She tried to put in her code a few times, and it almost locked her phone for a day. She handed me the phone and reminded me it was one-two-three-four. I mean, it was almost comical at how loud she said it, and everyone laughed, but no one cared. It's not like…"

"Like they could break into her phone and ask you where the key was?" Charlie said.

"Do you think that's what happened?" Gwyn looked hopeful for the first time in the interview.

"There's no way to know that for sure," Sophia reminded her, "but it's something we'll look into."

Charlie saw Gwyn's shoulders slump, and she wondered if this was her acting or her reality. Some of the best actors Charlie had seen could fool anyone if they believed what they were acting enough. Was this the case? Gwyn's role of a lifetime?

"Is there anything else you want to tell me?" Sophia held the edge of authority in her voice.

"No. I mean, just that I didn't do this. That wasn't me. Look though my stuff. You won't find anything of Katherina's there."

"We'll do that," Sophia said.

"Am I free to go?"

Charlie turned to Sophia to see what the woman would say. "We'll do that search and let you know."

Gwyn just nodded, and Sophia stood. Charlie followed suit. The detective closed the door once they were in the hall and turned to Charlie. "What do you think?"

"That she's an actress and I don't know if we can believe her or not."

"I had the same thought...though, while I did go hard at her, I'm not sure that she was lying," Sophia admitted.

"I got the same feeling. She did offer up a search quickly as well. Do you think that indicative of innocence, or that she's placed the jewelry elsewhere?"

"Could go either way." Sophia flipped her notepad closed. "I want to confirm this text message thread with Katherina. I find it odd she wouldn't have mentioned the request."

"Agreed." Charlie's phone buzzed and she saw another message from Ramona about a meeting of the crime club. She allowed a small smile, which the detective noticed.

"What is it?" Sophia asked.

"Nothing," Charlie said, waving farewell before she headed out the door and back to the Pearl Sands.

CHARLIE ARRIVED with food from *La Cantina*. Chips with salsa and queso, black bean taquitos, chicken empanadas, and churros for those with a sweet tooth. She'd had to have her taxi wait while she picked up the order at the southern end of the tied island, but it was worth it to see the eyes of her friends when she walked in with the amazing-smelling food.

"Perfect, I haven't had lunch yet," Valentina said.

Stephen eyed the chips and queso with something close to obsession. "I'm starving."

"Help yourself," Charlie said. She arranged the takeout containers on the table and brought out paper plates.

Ramona took one of everything and giggled like a schoolgirl. "This looks delicious."

Charlie didn't know much about the woman, but she knew that she spent most of her time at the Pearl Sands waiting for her husband, Sigmond, to come and join her.

She rented out her villa by the month and never seemed to consider doing anything else. She had expensive taste but didn't flaunt it. Her clothing was high quality but still functional. There was more beneath the surface of her friend that Charlie couldn't wait to get to, but for now, they had a case to discuss.

When they all had their food and were seated, Charlie hesitated. Nelson still hadn't arrived and, while he'd texted to say he'd be late, it was almost twenty minutes since the meeting time.

"Should we start without him?" She looked around the group.

"We can begin and then fill him in on the important things," Stephen said.

Charlie nodded and told them what Gwyn had said at the police station. How she'd assured them it had to be someone else who had texted her using Katherina's phone.

"But to follow that logic, whoever had gotten the answer and subsequently deleted the messages—so we assume—had to find a way into Gwyn's room." Stephen popped a queso-laden chip in his mouth after he finished.

Charlie nodded. "Good point. Valentina, do you think it could be likely that a maid would let someone else into another person's room? I'm not accusing your staff. Just curious how likely it might be."

"I'd say highly unlikely. I vet all new staff after their training and run them through scenarios just like this. They are trained to send people to the front desk no matter what."

"I see." Charlie had thought as much, but it was good to have confirmation.

"However, if someone they didn't know was entering the room, they wouldn't stop them. You can't know if someone has given out a key to their room."

"That's a good point," Charlie conceded. "I can check with the front desk, but they, too, are very good about not giving out random keycards. So, it's either a person who stole a card to get into the room or who she gave a key too."

"Wouldn't she have mentioned giving the key to someone?" Ramona asked.

"True. With the type of boss Katherina is turning out to be, I wouldn't be surprised to find she'd have a key to Gwyn's room and, if that's the case, if someone was close enough to use her phone, they might have been close enough to take Gwyn's extra key." Charlie felt the guess, which was what it really was, was a probable one, at least.

"It really sounds like you're saying that someone who is part of Katherina's group, for lack of a better term, is behind the theft." Ramona looked at Charlie for confirmation. "But not Gwyn."

"It seems likely. But it's more than that." Charlie tried to put her thoughts in order. "I think there is some strategy going on here, but perhaps not in the way we'd thought. Rather than discrediting Katherina, it seems to be just using Gwyn as a scapegoat, while the real objective is the necklace, or all the jewelry."

"So, money," Stephen said.

"Exactly." Charlie nodded as the thought took shape and grew roots. "They are using the premier week as a distraction. It's high profile, and there is a lot of confusion, but it's also not Katherina's home."

"What do you mean?" Valentina asked.

"It's as if someone has used this premiere week to their best advantage. They learned about the hotel, the security here—because the lights went off in the garden *and* the security office—and they are accomplishing their goals before the week is up." Charlie's thoughts flew even faster. "They took Ramona's jewelry as well and maybe another guest's. This is their endgame."

"Another guest?" Ramona interjected.

"Yes." Charlie berated herself for not checking in with them yet. "I heard about it while in the security office. I need to introduce myself, but it's just been one thing after the other."

"That's it, then? The objective is just robbery?" Valentina said.

"You sound disappointed," Ramona pointed out.

"It's not that. It just seems so coincidental."

"If it helps, I didn't find any new gossip in my searches," Stephen said. "None that would be relevant, I think."

"What did you find?" Charlie asked.

He shrugged. "There are rumors about Gwyn sleeping her way to the top, Katherina is getting a nose job, Elliot is planning some exclusive getaway and being secretive about it, and Thornton could be looking to acquire a new face in his agency."

Charlie knew most of the news was speculation or pure gossip, but Elliot had been secretive about his trip. Was it possible there was a bigger reason behind that? The fact he'd been looking into Cuba and Nelson had info from there hadn't escaped her notice.

"I'd hoped I might find something that showed someone was unhappy or out for revenge, but it really seems like, overall, Elliot Armstrong is a nice guy who doesn't like the limelight, and Katherina Kent's career is going strong —despite the nose job." He chuckled at his own joke. "Even if she doesn't get that new movie deal you'd mentioned, Charlie, Katherina has several others, if the gossip is to be believed. She's not hurting for parts."

"Which makes it all the more clear that Gwyn likely isn't behind the theft," Charlie surmised. "That's not proof, of course, but if she really isn't competing with Katherina, then why try to make her look bad?"

"She wouldn't." Ramona wiped at the corner of her mouth with a paper napkin. "In my conversation over dinner with Katherina last night, she didn't appear to be too worried about Gwyn as competition. She was worried that her assistant had taken advantage of her goodwill, but nothing beyond that."

"Then who's left?" Valentina said.

"Someone from the movie we haven't considered?" Ramona asked.

"Perhaps." Charlie was cut off from saying more by a quick knock on the front door before it opened to reveal Nelson.

"Sorry I'm late, everyone." He looked as tired—or more so—than Felipe, but Charlie had a feeling that had nothing to do with this case. "But I come with some good news."

"Tell us." Valentina clapped her hands in excitement before reaching for another chip.

"I heard back from my contact." Nelson took a seat, snatching a taquito first. "He says that there is a deal set up with a buyer he knows. Someone named Fernando. Said that Fernando said his contact goes by E. Strong."

The name fell heavy in the silence between them all.

E. Strong.

Elliot Armstrong.

13

THEIR DISCUSSION HAD COME to a standstill after cycling through all the ways in which it made sense—and didn't make sense—that Elliot Armstrong was the one behind the theft of the necklace. According to Stephen's research, he was worth millions, but how reliable could an internet search be?

From Charlie's observations, she never would have guessed that the man was hurting financially, or if he was, that he'd take the drastic action to steal his co-star's jewelry in order to get the money. Was it possibly about something else?

She had shared the brochure about Cuba and ziplining and how Elliot had acted strangely when she'd seen it. It was the only thing about him that hadn't seemed sincere.

Finally, when it felt more like they were spinning their wheels and less that they were gaining ground, she sent everyone off. Ramona was going to check in on the gossip surrounding Elliot from the other stars she'd become acquainted with, Valentia was going to check with the maids working on Katherina's floor, and Stephen was going back to teach a class. He felt bad he couldn't help more, but Charlie had told him honestly how his insight had been helpful.

Now, it was only Charlie and Nelson that remained of the crime club, and he dug into the leftover food like a starving man.

"Did you miss breakfast?"

"And dinner last night," he said, stuffing another empanada into his mouth. "And maybe lunch before that."

She didn't respond and, when he looked up, compassion washed through her at the haunted look behind his eyes. He was a man tormented by memories and while she didn't know what that was like with regards to a spouse, she did know what loss felt like.

"You're not okay, are you, Nelson?" Her thoughts traveled back to what Sophia had told her.

Surprise registered, but he looked down. "I know, the grease isn't the best idea."

"That's not what I mean, and you know it."

He shrugged. "It's been a rough…month."

"Do you want to talk about it?" Charlie held her breath. Would he finally open up to her?

He sat there, staring into the empty plate of empanadas until he took a deep breath and looked up to meet her gaze.

"You're right. I'm not okay."

Charlie wanted to say something to encourage him to keep talking, but she sensed that silence would be better. She kept her lips pressed together and waited.

"I told you about it being my—our—anniversary when we were at *La Cantina.*"

She nodded.

"And it is that, but it's so much more." He rubbed his face. "I know Sophia has talked to you a little, she mentioned that to me, and I don't care. I mean, it was her sister I was married to, but I also assume she hasn't told you everything. Right?"

"Correct. She only told me that it was going to be the ten-year anniversary of Gabriella's...murder."

The name seemed to impact him like an asteroid had hit. He imploded, shoulders hunching and head dropping. "Yes."

"I'm so sorry, Nelson."

He shook his head. "It's so much all at once, you know?"

She nodded. She did know.

He pulled back, almost as if forcing himself to, and faced her. "It's been ten years, and this story is still hard to tell, but I want to tell you what happened."

Charlie held his gaze. "Are you sure?"

His pained expression softened almost imperceptibly. "Yes. You've been a good friend to me, Charlie. Perhaps better than I deserve. I think it would help me to share it, if you're all right with that?"

"Of course." Charlie had the time, and she relished finding a way to help her friend.

Nelson dropped his gaze to the laminate flooring of the cottage and seemed to drop into a memory.

"I met Gabby after I'd left the Army—at the race, as I'd said." He flashed a smile. "She was a spitfire. Much like her sister. She was a high-powered lawyer, but I didn't know that when we first met. She just kind of rushed into my life like the perfect storm and I fell. Hard."

Charlie could imagine it. For all the experience he had as a CID officer, he had an artistic soft side as well, which made him a good potter.

"We started dating and got married and had a whirlwind life. She was busy with her career, and I was building my pottery business. At first, I was ashamed at the fact my wife was supporting me while I honed my craft, but she always told me she believed that I would make it. That the hard work would count for something later. I guess she was right."

"You're very talented, and she wanted to cultivate that in you." Charlie smiled at the thought. She would have liked Gabriella, that much was clear.

"We'd been married almost eight years when she came home one day and said that someone had passed her a note at the courthouse saying they knew who she was. She was a criminal defense attorney, and I took any threats to her very seriously, but she said she didn't feel threatened, just intrigued."

Charlie knew she would have felt the threat Nelson mentioned as well.

"We looked into it, but nothing came of it. I passed it off as nothing, but that was a mistake." Nelson dropped his head against his open palm. "I should have known… You can't have a past and expect it not to catch up with you."

"What do you mean?"

"You know I was with CID, and there were a few cases that, while they were military based, hit close to home. One in particular involved a high-ranking Army official caught colluding with smugglers to bring drugs into the United States."

Charlie's stomach constricted. There was corruption everywhere, that was no surprise, but to know that it was within their own military was even more tragic.

"We'd closed the case years ago, it was an older one I'd worked, but apparently, the man I put in jail through our investigation had a son. A son that had ties to the cartel.

He saw me dropping off Gabby one day at the courthouse and knew who I was. I'd gone with a superior to speak to the wife on behalf of the Army, because the family really is a victim as much as any other."

Charlie nodded. "That was the right thing to do."

"It was, and I stand by the action, but the son saw me there and latched on to me. In his child's mind, he thought I was the reason he no longer had a daddy. He had to leave base housing and their life changed drastically. I only learned later that his mother had committed suicide a few years after, and he was put into the foster system. It was a mess."

"So, he recognized you."

"Yes. From what I understand, he was handpicked by the cartel. They put him through law school, and he started to defend any members of or those associated with the cartel."

"So seeing you…"

"He used his influence. He…" Nelson swallowed. "He sent cartel members to follow Gabriella home one night, and they gunned her down right in front of our condo."

Now that the story was out, all emotion had leached from Nelson.

"I'm so sorry," Charlie whispered.

"I came out to the sound of the shots. She was just lying there. It was too late."

Charlie stood and came to perch next to him on the chair. She placed an arm around his shoulder and pulled him in for an awkward hug. He didn't need platitudes or to know it wasn't his fault—which it wasn't. He needed human contact. To know he wasn't alone in his grief.

"To this day, I know that it was the man's son who arranged all of this, but I've never been able to prove it. I did get a large bouquet of flowers delivered to our house signed with the name of the man I put away, which is what started me down the trail of what really happened." He took a shuddering breath. "I've told Sophia this. Time and time again, I've tried to prove to her who was behind Gabby's murder, but she's a woman of facts and can't see the whole picture. I mean, I suppose it does seem farfetched."

"But there's a connection."

"One only I can see. The boy's records were sealed, and I can't prove that Daniel Vena is the young boy whose father I sent to prison. His father has since passed away as well. But the worst part, the reason why I haven't eaten since yesterday, is the fact that *every* year on the anniversary of her death, I receive that same bouquet of flowers."

"That is sick." Charlie's muscles tensed.

"I've tried to track the sender, but the order is placed online from a public Wi-Fi and paid through a prepaid card. There's no way to trace it."

Charlie leaned back, her own frustration at the situation growing. "He's taunting you."

"Effectively, it would seem." Nelson met her gaze. "I took everything from him so he took my world from me."

A different emotion stirred in Charlie's chest. It was clear Nelson had loved his wife very much and, to him, she had been his world. Charlie wondered what that was like, but she pushed the thoughts aside. This wasn't about what she was thinking. This was about Nelson.

"What can I do?"

Nelson blinked. "Do?"

"Yes. Isn't that why you told me? You want my help to nail this man for the crime of hiring out your wife's murder?"

"I— I hadn't thought about that."

"You hadn't?" Charlie blinked.

"I just wanted to confide in someone who wouldn't question my story at every turn. Someone who could listen."

Charlie felt heat flood her cheeks. "I can do that, too."

"I know." Nelson took her hand and gently squeezed it. "That's why I told you."

"Thank you. For trusting me with this. I— I'm sorry. There are no words to make it better, but I'm grateful that you felt you could tell me."

"There aren't words," he agreed. "But having a friend I can rely on for the simplest of things to the more complex is worth it. We've only known each other a short time, and yet you know me so well. Thank you for being my friend."

As Nelson smiled, Charlie's brain did something funny. It made a connection she hadn't seen before. One brought on by Nelson's words, though she wasn't sure *how* they had been the trigger.

He narrowed his eyes. "You've got something, don't you."

She grinned and stood. "I do."

"But you're not going to tell me about it yet, are you?"

"Not yet, but you can do something for me."

"Yes?" She didn't miss the light of intrigue that entered his gaze.

"Have Elijah at the front desk send out an anonymous invitation to the cast of *A Night of Starlight* to meet in the small ballroom tonight. There is something that needs to be cleared up, and I think they'll all want to see it."

He stood, a man renewed. Whether it was from sharing his burden or the focus she'd offered him by giving him a task, she wasn't sure, but she liked seeing it.

"You've got it. And, Charlie?" He paused, waiting until he had her attention. "I'm always here if *you* need someone to confide in too."

There was a world of things she could think of that fit that bill, but she also knew that now wasn't the time for more sharing, it was a time for action, so she merely dipped her head in acknowledgement and raced out the door.

She had a clue to find.

———

"TONIGHT?" Sophia asked.

Charlie stood outside of the business center off the hotel lobby and tapped the toe of her shoe. "Yes. Tonight. Can you make it happen?"

"I— Are you sure about this?"

Charlie looked at the piece of paper in her hand. "Positive."

"Then I'll be there."

The detective hung up. Charlie had a lot of work to do, but first, she needed to make sure the pieces were laid out.

Folding the paper, Charlie slipped it into her pocket and sent a text to Juliana to see if she could cover Charlie's last shift. She hated to do it, but the woman's quick reply that the additional pay for the extra hours would be helpful alleviated Charlie's concerns.

Then, she put in a call to Stephen to ask for his expertise on gossip-hunting. With a few parameters for his search, he was off and running with a promise to send Charlie what he found as soon as possible.

Finally, she changed directions and went to speak with the most-recent victim, who Charlie hadn't met yet.

Olga Weathersby sat on the porch of her suite, looking out toward the shining water beyond. She had a wonderful view, and Charlie understood why her aide said she liked to spend most of her day out on the porch, either reading or watching the ocean.

"Hello, Mrs. Weathersby." Charlie stepped onto the porch through the sliding glass doors. It was one of the pie-shaped suites close to the garden on the bottom floor, and there were two chairs with cream-colored, comfy cushions suitable for outdoor use.

"Oh. Hello. Did we have a meeting?" Olga peered up at Charlie with a sweet smile.

"No, but I was hoping to speak with you for a few minutes about your missing necklace."

The sweet smile faded and was replaced by a scowl. "I've already spoken to that dreadful man, Mr. Simmons. I'd prefer not to speak on it again."

"I'm sorry about that, but he's with security. I'm... something different."

A thin eyebrow lifted. "Oh?"

Charlie explained who she was, what she did for the Pearl Sands, and then how she was also a PI.

"I love to hear that. A woman PI. Wonderful. I suppose it can't hurt to tell you the story, but I'll warn you that Mr. Simmons has already deemed me senile and ridiculous."

"I'm sure that's not true."

"No. He has. Told my aide as much while I was sitting *right here*. As if I'm deaf." She shook her head and let out a huff. "My hearing is perfect."

"Can you tell me what happened?"

"Certainly." Olga looked out to the ocean again.

The patio was slightly raised but still easily accessible from the ground. The height was just enough to make out the sail of a few ships out on the ocean and hotel guests enjoying the water on the hot afternoon.

"I don't bring my best jewelry on vacation. My late husband, Robert, always told me that. He was a good man." She seemed to slip into the past for a moment but recovered quickly. "I did bring one nice necklace, though. You see, I come on vacation to the same place every year. This is my first time at the Pearl Sands, though."

Charlie could tell by her tone that she wasn't convinced she'd be coming back. She made a mental note to send her a gift basket and an invitation to enjoy a spa item courtesy of the resort. Perhaps that would help soften the blow of Ben Simmons's attitude.

"Because I come to the same place, I always make time to see my friends here. I set up many coffee and lunch dates as well as a few dinners. The night the necklace went

197

missing—two nights ago, I believe—I went into town to have dinner with my friend Cybil. She's a sweet old gal, and we chatted well into the night for us, which means I was back by eight o'clock." She gave a tittering laugh, and Charlie couldn't help but smile. She liked Olga already.

"What happened next?" Charlie asked.

"My aide, Elizabeth, helped me dress for bed and then went to her adjoining room. I placed the necklace on the dresser there, because I was going to ask Elizbeth to return it to the vault the next morning. It's not worth *that* much, but it is something, you know?"

"Of course," Charlie encouraged.

"Then I went to sleep. When I woke up in the morning, the sliding door was ajar and my necklace was gone."

"Surely your aide could confirm she saw you had it with you."

"Oh yes, but they think I misplaced it somehow, even though they had maids in here looking into everything. I told them I'm not in the habit of leaving my door unlocked, but no one believes me."

Charlie looked around again and then turned to face Olga. "I believe you. I think your necklace was stolen, and I aim to find it for you, if I can."

Tears sprung to the older woman's eyes. "You are a dear." She sniffed. "You see, I wouldn't care so much if it hadn't been a necklace Robert gave me. I'll be fine without it, I'm not in need of the money, but it's the principle."

It was more than that, Charlie could tell. It was a piece of her she wanted back and deserved to have back.

"I'll do everything I can."

Olga looked back at her and shook her head. "You're a powerhouse, aren't you?"

Charlie merely laughed.

14

CHARLIE'S PHONE rang and she almost silenced it without looking but caught the contact info. "Felipe?"

"Hello. I… I cannot believe this, but I will not be there for the meeting." His voice was strained.

"What is it? Is something wrong?"

"It is my mother. She fell today. I must go to the facility and be with her."

"Of course. We've got it covered. Don't worry about anything."

"Are you…are you certain?"

Charlie allowed a small smile. "Positive. We're putting an end to the thefts tonight. I give you my word."

"Good. Then go get 'em. Isn't that what they say?"

She smiled. "It is. I hope your mother is all right."

"Me too." He was silent for a moment. "Thank you, Charlie. I will speak with you later."

She hung up just as Sophia entered the corridor. She made a beeline for Charlie and pulled her aside. The detective's wide brown eyes narrowed.

"We got a tip."

"Oh?" Charlie couldn't help but smile.

"Why does it look like you aren't surprised by this?"

"Because I'm not. I had a feeling something like this might happen."

"Are you going to fill me in?" Sophia planted her hands on her hips. "I don't like having to tell my officers to 'wait and see' when it comes to apprehending a thief."

"I agree, but I can't predict what will happen. I have a *feeling* I know some of how this will go down, however."

"I trust you, but this is asking a lot." Sophia's expression softened a little. "Come on, then. I'd better get this show on the road."

As per Charlie's request, Sophia burst into the room and took center stage, allowing Charlie to fade into the background. Katherina was at the center of it all, with Lars standing behind her against the wall with a wary eye to everyone else in the room.

To her right, she saw Gwyn, though she'd chosen to leave a chair between them in the circle of cushioned seats. She had her arms wrapped around herself. Next to her, Olga sat with an amused expression to be included in the bunch, and on her left sat Ramona. To the left of the main star, Thornton Blackwell sat with his legs crossed, Elliot next to him, Raji on his right, Hank Chambers, his assistant, and the makeup artist, Scarlett, completed the circle. It was everyone, plus Olga and Ramona, who had been in the vicinity when the lights went out at the garden party—just as Charlie had asked for.

"Before we begin, I have received a tip about one of you in this room." Sophia's voice echoed against the walls.

Charlie looked around the room but didn't see any obvious signs of discomfort, though that didn't surprise her. Whoever had organized this was someone who could be cool under pressure.

"Miss Milford, your purse, please."

"My— My purse?" Gwyn clutched it to her chest, eyes going wide.

"Please."

Then, as if making some decision, she thrust it outward. "You already searched my room, what could I be hiding?"

Sophia dug into the deep bag with a gloved hand and rummaged around. Charlie caught the moment Sophia found something. Her shoulders stiffened and she took a breath. "If that's true, then where did this red marker and tennis bracelet come from?"

She turned and showed the items that she'd found in Gwyn's bag.

"What? That isn't mine! I don't know how it got in there."

"That's my bracelet," Ramona said.

Charlie looked at the woman.

"There's a small sliver heart on one end, isn't there?"

Sophia checked and nodded. "There is."

That was a development that Charlie hadn't seen coming, but it worked in her favor.

"I'm afraid you're under arrest, Miss Milford." Sophia motioned for officers to take the woman away, though Charlie caught the detective's eye and knew they were on the same page.

"Can we go now?" Elliot asked.

"Not quite yet." Sophia made a circuit of the room, looking at each person. "You see, that was a little *too* coincidental. We are trained to pick up on things that seem too easy, and that fits the category."

"You've got the thief. What more do you need?" he asked. His shoulders were slumped, and it looked like was ready to leave.

"We need the *actual* thief," Charlie said. She stepped into the circle.

All eyes pivoted to her, and she introduced herself—even though everyone had already met her. "I'm Charlie Davis, and I work here at the resort. I'm also a licensed PI."

"So?" a female voice asked from behind her.

Charlie turned and saw the woman she'd yet to speak with. "It's Miss Watkins, correct?"

"Yeah." She folded her arms across her chest.

"I hear you are very skilled at what you do."

She shrugged.

"Mr. Chambers…" Charlie turned to the director. "Do you know Miss Watkins?"

"Who?" He looked up at her from where he'd been busy texting on his phone.

"Scarlett Watkins." Charlie didn't gesture to the young woman, merely dropped her name into the empty space he'd left.

"No. Never heard of her. Curt?" he asked the man next to him. The assistant, the same one Charlie had met at Hank's room, just shook his head. Hank said, "We don't know her."

Charlie went around the circle to the next person on her mental list. "Mr. White. Raji. How long have you known Elliot here?"

"We go way back." He grinned. "We were in kindergarten together."

"Is that right?"

"Yeah," Elliot supplied. "Remember what I said on the beach?"

"I do. And what does he do, exactly, for you again?" Charlie asked.

"He comes with me to shoots and sets and things like that. My righthand man, if you will."

"But he's not an assistant," Charlie clarified.

"No. He's a friend." Elliot's voice was firm.

Raji turned to him, and they bumped fists like they were teenagers.

"Where were you in between kindergarten and a few years ago?" Charlie asked Raji.

"Here and there. My parents moved around a lot for my dad's job."

"But you were fortunate to reconnect with Elliot," Charlie pressed.

"I was." He nodded.

"And, Elliot, tell me this. Are you planning a trip to Cuba soon?"

He immediately looked uncomfortable, his gaze skating around the room. "I— I'd prefer not to say."

The tension in the room shifted, and Charlie almost smiled. "I think you'd best, just so everything is out in the open here."

"Fine. Yes. We're going to Cuba."

"Who's 'we'?" She looked between him and Raji as if making a guess.

"Me, Raji, and his girlfriend." Elliot shrugged and ran a hand through his hair. He was still uncomfortable, but now Raji shifted his weight as well.

"Going to Cuba with Raji and his girlfriend. Tell me this, did you buy them the tickets?" Charlie faced Elliot.

"I— What does it matter?"

"Answer the question, Mr. Armstrong," Sophia said in her no-nonsense way.

"I did. So what? I try to help out Raji as much as I can. He doesn't make much from his freelance stuff, and I like to do what I can."

"You don't pay him to be around you?" Charlie turned to face Raji, meeting his gaze as if challenging him to defend Elliot. He said nothing.

"I tried at first, but he said it was enough that I just buy him lunch now and again and pay for the places we stay. Seemed fair to me, so that's how it's been." Elliot looked apologetically at Raji. "He doesn't like the spotlight so he does the behind-the-scenes stuff."

"Kind of you. And kind of you, Mr. White." Charlie leveled her gaze on Raji.

He looked up and locked eyes with her, his demeanor changing.

"Mr. White. You seem to be a helpful type of person." She paused, but he didn't move. "A great poker player. A good friend. And you help out on set. You've even helped Gwyn in the past with her work for Katherina. Isn't that right?"

"Yeah. So what?"

"So, on the day of the opening gala, you went into the business center to help out Gwyn with Katherina's speech cards. You printed them off and placed them in the podium. At least that's what you told me."

"And that's what happened." His expression didn't change, just his eyes narrowed slightly.

"What you failed to mention is that you printed out two copies of her speech."

She caught him swallow as his Adam's apple bobbed.

"One copy that was clear and the other that *you* marked with the red pen we just found in Gwyn's bag."

Elliot shot forward. "What are you talking about? He's my friend. He wouldn't do something like this."

"Is he really your friend, though?" Charlie turned to face Raji. "With a little help from a friend, Detective Perez was able to look into the past of Raji White. From the looks of it, he's living a great life in Canada, where his family moved shortly after school let out for the summer all those years ago. This man is not your best friend from childhood, but someone impersonating him."

"What? No way. Come on, tell her, Raji." Elliot turned to Raji, and there was something in the look the star gave Raji that told Charlie he'd had nothing to do with the plan she had slowly started to uncover.

"In fact, his name is Marcus Kaur, and he's wanted for burglary in the Chicago and Indianapolis areas." Sophia stepped up next to Charlie. "Thanks to your penchant for fancy drinks at the swim-up bar, I was able to grab your prints and run them through our system. You're under arrest, Mr. Kaur."

"I didn't do anything," he said, standing.

"Raji, tell them they're wrong. Come on, man, we've had crazy adventures for the last year. Tell them."

"He can't tell us because what we're saying is true. What friend doesn't know that his friend is allergic to alcohol? I'm sorry, Elliot, but Raji has been living a lie and not even *acting* like as good a friend as you thought."

Raji—really Marcus—merely sent Elliot a look and then allowed the officers to take him out of the room.

"So that's it? We can go?" Thornton leaned forward as if he wanted to get up and leave.

"Not yet." Sophia nodded back to Charlie.

"While Raji—that is, Marcus—is behind the thefts, there is more going on here than what I first thought." Charlie turned to look at those in the circle. "Like an accomplice."

Eyes widened, and everyone looked around the circle.

"We know everyone in this room. How would that be possible?" Hank asked.

"You don't *know* everyone. Take Miss Watkins, for example. She's supposedly well- known in the industry and has a reputation as being a talented makeup artist. She also had an invitation to the premier week, and yet you don't know her, Mr. Chambers."

"He's hardly an end-all, be-all to knowing everyone in the industry. And I don't have to take this." Scarlett stood and yanked her purse from the floor. "I'm out of here."

"No so fast," Sophia said, stepping into her path. "I did my due diligence and looked into your past, Miss Watkins. While it's true you *did* work in Hollywood for a time, you've been absent for more than a year now and no one has worked with you in that time. What have you been up to?"

"Private gigs. You know, doing makeup for the stars." Scarlett's cheeks were red.

"Anyone we'd know?" Charlie met her hard stare.

"I'm not at liberty to say."

"Miss Watkins, you're under arrest for robbery at the Pearl Sands, but also at least one home in town."

Scarlett's mouth gaped. "What?"

"You, too, have enjoyed a few cocktails here, which has made it easy for me to get your prints. When I ran them against the unknown print we found at a local crime scene, they matched."

"It seems you met Marcus and went into the lucrative business of cat burglary." Charlie shrugged. "It's a shame. Everyone I talked to said you had real talent."

Another officer came and took Scarlett away. Charlie turned back to the group.

"I couldn't understand why only Ramona and Olga's jewelry was taken. If you were a jewel thief, wouldn't you want to steal as much as you could? But then I realized that's exactly what you *wouldn't* want to do. You wouldn't want to overstretch and create a stir."

"Leave the main target my necklace is that what you're saying?" Katherina asked. She looked genuinely interested now.

"Yes," Charlie said.

"But why me?" Ramona asked.

Charlie turned to her friend. "I think you were a bit of a test run, but also an easy target." Charlie grimaced so her friend knew she wasn't saying it cruelly. "From what I understand, you took quite a bit off of Raji in poker and, while he still got some wins in, he was floundering. The theft was his way of getting his losses back."

"How would they know I wouldn't make a stink about it?" Ramona asked.

"I don't think they did, but it did work in their favor."

"What about me?" Olga said, looking from Sophia back to Charlie.

"You said you'd left your necklace out on the dresser, right?" Charlie asked. The woman nodded. "While this is unsubstantiated, I think that Scarlett got a taste for theft when—or after—she met Marcus, and your necklace was too much of a temptation. She'd already escaped from the garden party, using your room as her exit, and left by way of your balcony. She must have taken it on the way out—a bonus theft."

"I should have listened to my aide and sent it back to the vault that night," Olga said.

"It's not your fault," Sophia said. "Marcus and Scarlett planned this for a long time and were close to getting away with it."

"I don't understand. How...how is it possible? I thought he was Raji?" Elliot asked.

"I was wondering the same thing," Charlie said. "After my friend Stephen found the real Raji White, helped by Detective Perez, I called him up and we talked. He said that the man I described sounded a lot like a man he'd known by the name of Ajay. They worked at the same high-end restaurant in Toronto and became friends. He said they were always getting confused for one another because they looked alike—except for Ajay's dimples— and then he recalled very vividly that a commercial you'd done came on one day and he bragged that he'd known you."

"It was the car one, I bet." Elliot spoke as if in a trance.

"Raji said Ajay was extremely interested in knowing all about it and how you'd met and random details. Raji hadn't thought anything about it at the time, so he'd told Ajay everything he could remember. Then one day, Ajay quit, and he never heard from him again."

"So he came and found me and used all that information to get into my good graces. How did I fall for that?" Elliot dropped his head into his hands.

"Marcus is a skilled manipulator." Sophia faced the whole group now. "We don't know yet how he met Scarlett, but she was the key to getting this heist done here. Marcus had an in with you so she made her own way in, pulling some favors from past jobs, but they couldn't help themselves. They committed thefts in the area before even coming to the resort."

"Raji—or whatever his name is—said he wanted to come early to scope out the location for me. I-I believed him." Elliot shook his head.

"I'm inclined to believe this was their last big heist for a while. They tricked Elliot into getting them tickets on a private plane to Cuba, and we think they were going to ditch you there." Charlie offered a conciliatory smile to Elliot. "You were hesitant to share the details of your trip, and I thought that was because you were complicit, but it was something else, wasn't it?"

Elliot nodded. "I don't like telling anyone where I'm going. Too many times, fans have shown up and it takes away from a relaxing vacation. Raji—Marcus—fed into that. Told me this trip needed to be top secret so that we could finally get away from it all. I thought... I thought it was going to be a great time."

"But what about my jewelry?" Katherina asked. "And Gwyn?"

All eyes turned to her, but Charlie spoke up. "Gwyn likely had nothing to do with all of this, but we needed her out of the room for the time. Marcus offered to print out the copies of the speech for her and when he went to put them in the podium, he showed them to one of the security guards. They looked fine because it was the copy that was unmarked. He must have made the switch to the marked copies before he even left the room."

"As for the necklace," Sophia cut in, "we think once we check through Mr. Armstrong's baggage, we'll find it and the other jewelry. We think they will have covered their tracks, using Mr. Armstrong as a mule, just in case someone was to check their baggage."

"I'll get it back?" Katherina looked relieved.

"All of it," Charlie said. "I think that Scarlett impersonated Gwyn after either she or Marcus used your phone to get the location of the key. They are similar enough to look alike, and makeup can help a great deal with that."

"They planned it all and were almost going to get away with it." Thornton sounded shellshocked.

"Thankfully, they didn't." Sophia looked around. "Thank you all for coming and please be sure to keep these events to yourself for now. Our investigation is still ongoing, but we needed to ensure they didn't feel singled out."

Everyone stood to leave, but Katherina made a beeline for Charlie. "You did it, Ms. Davis. You found the thief, and I'm so grateful."

Charlie smiled. "It's my pleasure."

15

CHARLIE RAN her hand down the front of her new dress as she stood at the back of the ballroom. The silky feeling of the red material clued her in to its quality, but she couldn't help but smile. She felt elegant.

The dress had arrived on the doorstep of her cottage earlier that evening with a note from Felipe that she'd earned it and more with her efforts to unmask the thief in their midst. Normally, she wouldn't have accepted such a personal—and luxurious—gift from a man that she wasn't dating, but she sensed no ulterior motives. Only gratitude.

Despite the fact that the heels were low, they still pinched her toes, and she shifted from one foot to the other as the ballroom slowly filled with people. The premiere showing had ended fifteen minutes ago in another ballroom they'd turned into a theater, and now everyone was coming for the wrap-up of the week, awards, and dinner.

It felt a little like déjà vu being back in the South Sea Ballroom, but Charlie faced it with more excitement, since it meant the end of the grueling week of events. Besides, the team had totally transformed the area to reflect a roaring twenties theme, and it was perfect.

"There you are."

The gruffness of the voice tipped her off to who it was before she turned around. "Hello, Ben."

He nodded once at her. "You look nice."

His compliment surprised her. "Thank you."

"Look." He nailed her with a hard stare. "I think I've been wrong about you."

Charlie tried but failed to hide her astonishment.

"I know we seem at cross-purposes sometimes—me working from a security angle and you from, well, I don't know if it's a PI angle or a concierge one—but either way, we are going after the same thing."

"Which is?"

"Stopping the bad guys. I know—" He held up a hand. "—that sounds more superhero than I wanted it to, but you get what I'm saying."

"I do." She nodded.

"Good." He took a deep breath. "You were right."

"I'm going to need more than that, Mr. Simmons."

He barely contained a grin. "I looked into the problem of the security office power going out and found the weak link. One of my newly hired guys admitted to disclosing information he shouldn't have when a pretty girl offered to buy him a few drinks."

"Scarlett," Charlie guessed.

"He admitted it was her when I showed a photo. He's no longer employed here, and...you were right."

"Be careful, Mr. Simmons, or I could get used to you telling me that."

Now, he laughed. "Don't worry. It doesn't happen often. And please, call me Ben."

Charlie gauged his intentions, but she came away feeling as if he'd been nothing but honest with her. "And you can call me Charlie."

He nodded once and turned to go before pausing to say, "I think we could make a good team."

"I think we already do."

His smile was the only reply.

Charlie turned back to observing, although the new connection with Mr. Simmons—*Ben*—surprised her. He wasn't someone she'd have guessed to be interested in making nice, but she wasn't beyond making allies wherever possible. If Ben could be that with her here at the resort, she'd take it.

"You look like a star." Valentina and Stephen came up to her, both decked out in another stunning dress and tux, respectively.

"As do you two." Charlie smiled widely. "Did you enjoy the movie?"

"Absolutely." Valentina looked as if she still had stars in her eyes.

"It was all right," Stephen admitted.

"He'd rather watch true crime documentaries." Valentina rolled her eyes.

"But the acting was good," he capitulated.

"Nice of Felipe to let you guys watch," Charlie observed.

"He said it was the least he could offer us for helping you." She shrugged. "We really didn't do that much, but he insisted."

Charlie kept her mouth closed, but she knew exactly why Felipe had thought that. She'd made it clear that she hadn't done what she did alone. She liked to give credit where credit was due.

"Are you staying for the dinner?" Charlie asked.

"Are you crazy?" Stephen kept his voice low, but his eyes widened. "It's over seven hundred dollars a plate."

"I'll take that as a no." Charlie covered her laugh with a hand.

"We just wanted to see you," Valentina said, "and to say thanks for including us. Maybe next time, we can do even more."

Charlie swallowed at the words. Next time? She hoped there was never another time that a thief was left to run rampant through the Pearl Sands, but she just shrugged. "We'll see."

"We're off to *La Cantina*. See you later, Charlie!" Valentina pulled Stephen by the arm.

She watched her friends go with a pang of regret. She'd volunteered to keep an eye on things at the banquet so that Juliana could go to her niece's school play and party. While she didn't regret helping her, Charlie didn't *want* to be here.

She'd seen enough of Hollywood to last her a lifetime.

"I LIKE LARGE PARTIES. They're so intimate."

Charlie whirled around to see Nelson making his way across the patio. He wore a tux with a white shirt and white bowtie and walked with confidence.

"Isn't that a line from *The Great Gatsby*?"

"That it is." He held up a martin glass and toasted her. She laughed.

"It felt it appropriate for tonight. You look radiant, by the way." Nelson's gaze intensified with the compliment, but he only looked into her eyes.

"Thank you. I'm about ready to shuck these shoes, though."

He laughed. "Shuck away."

She did and her height dropped as her feet alighted on the cool tile. She let out a sigh of relief. "That is so much better."

"You've been here for hours," he observed.

"I've been making sure everything goes smoothly. Aside from a few little hiccups with the wrong meals going to the wrong guests, and a few other small incidents, it's been a quiet night."

Behind them, through the open double-doors, they could see guests dancing. Loud music flowed out, though the sound of ocean waves dulled it some out here. The night itself was still warm and a bit humid, but overall, it was pleasant.

"I'd say everything was a success. Including the wrap-up of the mysterious thief—excuse me, *thieves.*" He grinned down at her.

"How did you hear about that? Wait, let me guess, the crime club? Sophia?"

He mimicked locking his lips and throwing away the key. "I'm glad, though, that it's over."

"Me too." Her shoulders relaxed. "They searched Elliot's luggage and, just as Sophia guessed, everything was in there in hidden compartments. Katherina has all her jewels again as does Ramona and Olga. Everything's back to the way it should be."

"And yet you're out here avoiding the celebration." He shifted to lean against the stone railing.

"Do you know me at all?" She laughed, making it clear the words were a joke.

"Why do you think I'm out here too?"

Her forehead winkled.

"I was looking for you. Felipe said I could find you out here."

His words surprised her. She'd spoken briefly with the hotel manager after the wrap-up and his return to work the next day. It was clear his mind was on his mother and not the resort, but she'd dutifully filled him in and left him to his thoughts.

"I feel bad for him."

"Why?" Nelson frowned before taking another sip of his drink.

"His mother had to have surgery on her hip from a fall, and he's got all of this to deal with. It's a lot, and I don't know if his boss realizes that." Charlie let out a breath. She needed to tread carefully, because she didn't want her judgment of a man she'd never met to come out without a foundation. She was grateful for her job and never wanted it to seem otherwise.

"You think he shouldn't be working." Nelson said it as a statement.

"I think he needs time off that he won't take."

"I see." Nelson nodded. His gaze traveled through the darkness. "You think he can't get the time, then?"

She looked up, sure her genuine concern for the man was plain on her features. "I don't know. I just know that it's hard to care for a parent *and* work a job well."

Nelson's expression softened. "Do you care for him?"

Charlie was thankful for the darkness as her cheeks heated. "What?"

"You know a lot about him. Perhaps more than I do, and I've known him a long time. I'm just curious."

Her stomach constricted. This wasn't the conversation she'd expected to have with Nelson tonight. If anything, it was a conversation she'd wanted to have with Felipe first, but Nelson had beaten her to it.

Charlie squared her shoulders and debated the best approach. She could beg off and not answer the question —though that could be seen as an answer itself—or she could be honest.

Honesty always won for her.

"I don't. Not in the way you're saying. I thought I might. We've gone on a few dates, and he's an honorable, kind, and compassionate man, but…"

"There's no spark?" Nelson guessed.

"That and the fact that I don't think he has room in his life for me. Perhaps I don't have room in my life for him either—at least not like that."

Stars reflected in the depths of Nelson's eyes as he looked down at her. He set his martini glass on the stone next to them, and Charlie found her breaths coming shallowly. Nelson had an intensity about him that had put her off at first, but now she faced the full weight of it and wasn't sure what she felt.

It was like standing on the edge of a deep pool. She could easily walk away, or she could dive in.

"Nelson."

"Charlie."

They spoke at the same time, and Nelson's lips curled up into a smile.

He spoke first. "There are things I want to say to you, but I don't trust myself. Not that what I want to say isn't true, but I don't trust myself to say it right. To feel it." He placed a hand over his heart. "This month is always hard for me, and you've proven that you're willing to walk through that alongside me. That means so much, but I wonder if it's clouding my judgment."

She watched as emotions played out over the planes of his face, the dark only enhancing his handsomeness.

"So, I can't say those things to you tonight." She caught a flicker of regret.

She thought she understood. He was still hurting from the murder of his wife. Still reeling from the reminder—the flowers—and from being vulnerable enough to tell her about it. Perhaps if he gave in and told her what he wanted to, he worried he might regret it. Words spoken in the heat of a moment, not in cool rationality.

That was something she could understand.

It was her turn to be vulnerable. "I understand. And no, I'm not just saying that. What you said the night of the gallery opening was partially accurate. There is still a lot about me you don't know, and I'm not sure I can tell you all of it, but perhaps one day, I can."

Her words mirrored his own, but they seemed to be exactly what he needed to hear.

"I think there's a world of things between us we won't talk about, but maybe we should someday." He took her hand, slowly pulling it to his lips and kissing her knuckles. "But for now, let's agree to one thing."

She tried and failed to ignore the way his lips sent shockwaves through her. "What's that?"

"Let's agree to put our friendship first."

It wasn't what she wanted, down deep in her heart, but it was best—for them both. For now.

She flashed a smile. "Deal."

"Arturo, this is the best coffee I've ever had."

The hearty laugh of Sophia's husband echoed through the kitchen. He wore gray jersey shorts and a neon blue tank top, his feet in sandals as he came around the counter. "I'm glad you like it. Help yourself to what's left in the French press." He winked at her and walked toward the other side of the house, pausing to kiss Sophia on the lips before disappearing down the hall.

"That man is worth his weight in gold." Sophia took a long sip of her own coffee.

They took their mugs out to the screened-in patio, a ceiling fan blowing down onto them to alleviate some of the heat of the morning.

"I'd hoped it would be cooler this early, but not today." She pressed a button on the remote and the speed of the fan kicked up.

"I've got to say, I'm shocked to be sitting here." Charlie peered over at the detective from behind her excellent cup of coffee. "At the home of the infamous Detective Perez."

"Here's the thing, Charlie..." Sophia set her mug down and faced her. "I was wrong. Yes, we've established that, but I mean *really* wrong. About you."

"Thanks?"

Sophia grinned. "I told Arty after you and I first met that you were going to be my nemesis, but now I've realized you're something more than that."

Charlie's eyes narrowed. "What's that?"

"You're my friend. And friends come over for coffee on Sunday mornings, friends talk about things other than murder and burglary, and friends are there for one another." She was silent for a moment.

Tears pressed against the back of Charlie's eyes, and she willed them away. "Is that what friends do?"

"I think so." Sophia barked a laugh. "Being a woman cop— and a detective at that—has made it hard to make true friends. That sounds like an excuse, but I have a feeling you know what I mean. But working this case with you has been, dare I say, fun? You're good at what you do, but more than that, I look forward to talking with you in general. I figure, why leave that to chance? Why not become friends instead."

"I like the sound of that." And Charlie did. She knew exactly what Sophia was talking about. Even being a woman private investigator, she'd found herself isolated, and she'd made this move to the island and resort to change that.

Sophia beamed. "I know you're still kind of new to town and, when that was me in the past, I always wanted someone to reach out. Someone to invite me to their home, because I hate being the new woman in town. I wanted to do the same for you. I know you've lived here for a while now, and you have other friends, but I wanted to give you a space you could come to that was off the island, if you wanted. Is that too much?"

Charlie laughed. "Not at all. I appreciate it."

"Good." A conspiratorial gleam entered her eyes. "Because, despite the fact you keep telling me you're just a concierge, I'm pretty sure you're the unofficial PI of the Pearl Sands Resort."

Charlie opened her mouth to disagree, but Felipe's words about her involvement came back to her followed by her first civil conversation with Ben. Maybe what everyone was trying to tell her was true.

She could be a concierge *and* maintain her PI license.

Instead of refuting Sophia's words, she just smiled, took another sip of her coffee, and said, "Maybe you're right."

Thanks for reading *Theft in the Theater*. We hope you enjoyed this adventure with Charlie, the Pearl Sands Resort, and, of course, Cal the mischievous monkey. If you could take a minute and leave a review for me on Amazon and/or Goodreads, that would be really nice :)

The next book in the Pearl Sands Beach Resort Cozy Mystery series will be released soon. Keep an eye out for it on Amazon.

Also, be sure to check out the Florida Keys Bed and Breakfast Cozy Mystery series where we first met Charlene. The first book in that series is called *Murder Mystery Book Club* and it has over 2400 five star reviews on Amazon (and over 4800 total reviews).

If you would like to know about future cozy mysteries by me and the other authors at Fairfield Publishing, make sure to sign up for our Cozy Mystery Newsletter. We will send you our FREE Cozy Mystery Starter Library just for signing up. All the details are on the next page.

FAIRFIELD COZY MYSTERY NEWSLETTER

Make sure you sign up for the Fairfield Cozy Mystery Newsletter so you can keep up with our latest releases. When you sign up, **we will send you our FREE Cozy Mystery Starter Library!**

FairfieldPublishing.com/cozy-newsletter/

Made in the USA
Middletown, DE
19 February 2025

71571049R00139